INDIAN LEADER
LEADER
TRAIL BOSS

INDIAN LEADER
LEADER
TRAIL BOSS

CLARK SELBY

Author ReputationPress®
Creativity & Branding

Author Reputation Press LLC
45 Dan Road Suite 36
Canton MA 02021
www.authorreputationpress.com
Hotline: 1(800) 220-7660
Fax: 1(855) 752-6001

Ordering Information:
Quantity sales. Special discounts are available on quantity purchases by corporations, associations, and others. For details, contact the publisher at the address above.

Printed in the United States of America.

ISBN-13:	Softcover	978-1-951020-32-3
	eBook	978-1-951020-33-0

Library of Congress Control Number: 2019911573

This book is dedicated to my wife, Karen Serene Selby, for her love and for editing and supporting my writing, and for being the inspiration for my book's heroine.

CONTENTS

CHAPTER ONE

TROUBLE GETTING TO WORK

INDIAN LEADER WAS APPROACHING another little Texas town, like a hundred other little towns he had rode into, dark, dusty, and windblown. God, Indian hated that damn wind; he had so much dust and dirt in his clothes and saddlebags that he thought his horse must be carrying an extra hundred pounds.

Indian saw a light on at the local watering hole and headed his horse straight for it. As he stepped down from his horse, Tomahawk, a man came busting out of the saloon and yelled, "I hate the way you look, cowboy!"

The man drew his gun and fired at Indian; Indian fell to the ground and pulled his Colt and aimed at where he'd seen the flash of the man's gun.

The man fired his gun again as he was falling down on the dusty street.

Several people rushed out of the saloon as Indian stood over the man lying on the ground.

Indian's Colt was still at the ready in case there was more trouble.

When Indian saw there wasn't anyone else trying to kill him, he turned to the people from the saloon and asked, "Who in the hell is this man?"

One of the men stepped forward and replied, "His name is John Phillips."

Indian asked, "Do you know why he wanted to kill me?"

The same man answered, "I don't think he was trying to kill you. He'd been drinking all day and had threatened everybody in the place. When no one would answer his challenge, he ran out of the saloon, yelling he was going to kill the first son of a bitch he saw. Reckon you were the first one he saw."

Indian said, "That's a hell of way to be greeted in a town I've never be in."

About that time the local sheriff came wandering over and asked, "What's going on here?"

The same man who had been talking to Indian said, "That crazy kid, John Phillips, tried to pick a gunfight with everybody in the saloon, and when no one would take him up on it, he went storming out of the saloon, yelling he was going to kill the first person he saw. Reckon this stranger was the first one he saw, but I guess he didn't pick the right someone."

The sheriff turned to Indian and asked, "What's your story, fellow?"

Indian said, "I rode into town and was getting off my horse when this fool busted out of the saloon, yelling he didn't like the way I looked and reached for his gun and fired a shot at me.

"So I fell to the ground, pulled my gun, and shot him before he had another chance to shoot me. That's my story."

The sheriff asked, "What's your name, stranger?" "My name is Indian Leader."

Neither the folks gathered outside the saloon nor the sheriff had ever seen Indian Leader before, but everybody in Texas knew who he was. He was the most famous trail boss in Texas, and he was the only trail boss who had never lost a herd and never lost a man on a trail drive. He was somebody every cowboy who'd ever been on a trail drive talked about in every saloon in Texas.

Most everyone who ever told stories about Indian Leader always told how he dressed and about his gun rig; he was always dressed in buckskin and had a fancy hand-tooled leather holster with his Colt 44 at his right side and a matching leather holster made for a cross draw on his left side with another Colt 44 in it.

The man the sheriff was staring at was dressed just like the stories he had always heard about Indian Leader except he didn't have the second Colt in the cross-draw holster he had heard about.

The sheriff said, "You don't look like any Indian I ever saw. You got straw-colored hair."

"That's because I'm not an Indian. That's my name. I'm English and Irish. My folks named me that because I was born in the Territory."

"What are you doing in Cedar City?"

"I'm on my way to the Star Ranch in DeWitt County to pick up a herd of Longhorns headed for Dodge City. They lost a couple of herds this year, so they contacted me to see if I could get one through for them."

The sheriff said, "Well, I guess that's about all. Mr. Leader, you can go on your way, but you need to keep your guard up 'cause his seven elder brothers aren't going to be happy about losing their youngest brother. If I was you, I'd make a wide loop around Cedar City from now on if you want to have a future.

"The Phillips are bad people to have problems with. You can ask anybody who ever dealt with them. They've killed a lot of men for no reason, and you will be on the top of their list for killing their baby brother."

"Thanks for the advice, Sheriff. I'll be on my way as soon as I have a drink and something to eat. Been riding a long time, and I need a drink and some food before I push on."

"Just the same, Leader, I'd get away from here as quick as you can before the Phillips boys come to town, 'cause they're going to be coming after you. They're troublesome, mean hombres, as soon shoot you as to look at you!"

"Thanks again, Sheriff."

By the time Indian came out of the saloon, the undertaker had taken the body of John Phillips away. Out of habit, Indian took a long look in both directions before mounting his horse.

He didn't need any trouble with the Phillips brothers because he would have enough trouble trying to get a herd of three thousand head of Longhorn cattle to Dodge City, Kansas; no sir, he didn't need something else to worry about.

Indian headed his horse south out of Cedar City as fast as he could toward DeWitt County to meet the owner of the Star Ranch and make arrangements to take their herd of Longhorns to Dodge City.

The biggest problem he had to worry about was it was really late in the year to make a trip up the Great Western Trail to Dodge City. Nobody, including him, could tell if there was going to be an early winter snowstorm, making it impossible to get a herd through without losing most of them.

Indian thought it was too damn late in the year to make this drive, but he was stupid enough to try for somebody who really needed his help. And Mr. Star needed his help.

Those storms had been known to wipe out whole herds and cost the lives of all the cowboys driving them. It was already August, and it would take Indian another three weeks' riding before he got to the Star Ranch.

Indian thought, "First things first." He better get out of Cedar City before he had to tangle with the seven Phillips brothers. He didn't like killing people, and he had already had to kill somebody he had never even seen before. He didn't want to have to kill any more of the Phillips.

The thought never crossed his mind that they might kill him. Before he began trail-bossing, he was a deputy sheriff in St. Louis County, Missouri, and he had been involved in far too many gunfights. He didn't use his real name back when he had that job.

He didn't want to become known as a lawman, because once you were you known as a lawman, you could never get out of the job, and if you had a reputation as a quick draw, you became a target for every gunslinger in the west trying to prove how fast they were.

Back then he went by the name Johnny Able and was considered to be one of the fastest drawing lawman in Missouri— some said, maybe in the west.

Indian wanted to be as far away from that reputation as he could get.

Becoming a trail boss let him get away from all of that; now he had a great reputation as one of the best trail bosses in Texas, and no one he had ever met in this job knew his past. Besides, he was older now, so he didn't look like the fresh-faced kid when in worked in St. Louis.

He put Tomahawk on a trot when he rode out of Cedar City. He would stay on the trail toward San Antonio as long as he could before turning southeast toward DeWitt County.

Indian was several miles away from Cedar City before he slowed Tomahawk to an easier pace.

Since nothing happened after a week went by he thought maybe the Phillips brothers might not be trying to come after him after all. He hoped he was right; maybe after the Phillips heard about what happened to their brother, they would forget trying to take revenge on him. At least that was his hope.

Hope was a great thing. "We all need hope," he said to himself. "Everybody needs hope."

Indian found a nice place to bed down for the night next to a small stream and made himself a nice fire to cook supper with. Later that night he heard a couple of horses approaching his camp. Even from the light of his campfire he could see these horses had been pushed hard for some time.

Indian said, "Howdy! You fellows want to step down and join me for some coffee?"

One of the men replied, "Don't mind if we do."

Indian kept watching as the two men stepped down from their mounts, and he said, "Looks like you fellows have been riding pretty hard. What's your hurry?"

The man who spoke earlier replied, "We're trying to catch up with a fellow who killed our brother."

Indian slowly replied, "Your name's not Phillips, is it?" Both men replied, "Yes."

Indian stood up and stepped away from the fire and said, "I guess you found the man you're looking for. Listen, I don't want any trouble with you two. Just get on your horses and go home. I didn't want to kill your brother. He didn't give me much choice since he shot at me first."

The two men didn't reply to Indian. They both reached for their guns, but before either one of their guns cleared their holsters, Indian pulled his Colt from his right holster and shot both of them.

Indian quickly walked over to where the two men fell and took away their guns and watched their horses run away after his shots were fired.

One of the men was dead; the other one was alive, but badly hurt. Indian knew he wouldn't make it through the night. Blood was pouring from his chest. Indian laid the wounded man down with his head on Indian's saddle, trying to make him as comfortable as he could.

Indian tried to stop the bleeding, but the wound was too deep; he couldn't do much for him.

Indian got some water from the stream and tried to give the man a drink of it, but the best he could do was to rub some water on his lips. An hour later the man died.

The next morning, Indian buried both of the men, put their six-guns in his saddlebags, caught their two horses, unsaddled them, and turned them loose. He tied the men's Winchester rifles to his saddle rig and started riding south again.

It had been quite an evening and a long morning. Indian felt like he had done a day's work by the time he climbed up on his saddle and rode away from this place.

Before riding off he said a prayer for the two men he killed and asked God to forgive them and hoped this would be the end of the Phillips trying to kill him.

Indian didn't like killing people; he had seen far too much of useless killing in his life. He didn't like doing it even when it meant saving his own life.

He just hoped that this would be the end of the Phillips trying to kill him; he already had to kill three of them, but there were four more brothers left.

Indian still had two weeks of riding before arriving at the Star Ranch, and he didn't need any more trouble. He worried more about the weather every day; every night it already seemed to him that it was getting colder.

Indian arrived in Cuero, Texas, on September 6 and asked directions to the Star Ranch. He was told it was about ten miles west of town. The fellow said, "You can't miss it. Just ride west until you get there." Directions like that could really get you lost.

Indian was sure having trouble going to work at his new job.

CHAPTER TWO

SO THIS IS THE STAR RANCH

NDIAN RODE WEST FROM Cuero for what he thought must be about ten miles, but he couldn't tell if he was on the Star Ranch or not. Suddenly he heard a shot being fired, and he fell from his horse.

Indian lay very still as a cowboy got off his horse and walked up to where he lay. When Indian saw the toe of a boot headed straight for his head, he grabbed it, pulling the owner of the boot to the ground. He jumped to his feet and pulled his six-gun and pointed it at the cowboy lying on the ground.

Two other cowboys rode up about that time and Indian turned his attention to them as he continued to hold the man on the ground with his foot planted firmly on the man's neck.

One of the cowboys on a horse yelled out, "Hold on, Tex, don't shoot. We thought you were one of the rustlers."

Indian took his foot off the man's neck so he could get up and then calmly asked, "Is this the Star Ranch?"

The cowboy standing next to Indian said, "Yes, sir."

"If this is the Star Ranch, I'm here to see the owner. I'm Indian Leader!"

The cowboy standing next to him said, "I'm really sorry, sir. I'm Teddy Smith."

Indian put his gun back in its holster and stuck out his right hand and said, "It's all right, son. I'm just glad you're not a better shot."

The two cowboys on horses laughed loudly, got down from their horses, and introduced themselves; one said his name was Lloyd Johnson, and the second one was Toby Smith.

They both shook hands with Indian. Toby said, "I'm really sorry about my brother trying to shoot you, sir."

Indian replied, "I've had worse things happen to me. I need to talk with your boss man."

Toby replied, "Well, that's going to be pretty hard, because he got bushwhacked a couple weeks ago by rustlers. Guess you'll have to talk with the new boss lady."

"I'm sorry to hear about Mr. Ben Star. I've heard he was a good man. I guess you better take me to talk with your boss lady."

They mounted up, and the three cowboys led Indian to the ranch headquarters and straight to the ranch house.

On arriving at the ranch house, Teddy got down from his horse, walked up to the house, and knocked on the door. A few minutes passed before a young woman answered the door.

Teddy said, "Miss Star, Mr. Indian Leader is here to see you." Indian approached Miss Star and said, "Miss Star, I'm very sorry to hear about your father."

She replied. "Thank you. Come in, Mr. Leader."

Indian followed her inside the house. It was a pleasure following her; she was a beautiful young woman. Indian thought she was one woman he might like to spend some time with. In the past he never had much time for any woman in his life.

However, after taking a good look at Miss Star, he wondered if a woman like her would even be interested in spending time with him—probably not.

She must have every young man in southeast Texas chasing her and maybe a few old ones too.

Indian guessed she must be about twenty or twenty-five years old. She had long dark-brown hair and beautiful brown eyes. He thought she must be about five foot five. She had a beautiful face and a wonderful figure. She was truly a handsome young woman.

He thought that since her father had been killed, she would get her mother to talk with him; instead, she asked him to sit down at the desk, and she went around to the other side of the desk and sat down at the desk directly across from him.

She said, "Mr. Leader, my name is Serene Star. I'm the new owner of the Star Ranch, and I really need your help getting my cattle to market. We've already lost two herds on the way to market this year. If we don't get this herd through, I'm afraid I'm going to lose the ranch."

She continued, "My dad was a great cattleman but maybe not as good on the business side of running a ranch. He bought another section of land for the ranch that we didn't need and borrowed the money from the bank in Cuero to pay for it.

"As bankers go, they're nice folks, but we have to repay the loan by the first of February. We should have already paid off the bank, but losing those herds left us pretty broke. Can you help me?"

Indian swallowed hard and said, "I'll get your herd through for you, ma'am."

Serene replied, "Thank goodness you're here. Everybody else thinks we don't have a chance. They say the Star Ranch is jinxed, and with a woman boss, it's the kiss of death."

She continued, "After my mother died, my dad sent me back east to go to school to learn about business. He wanted me to be able to help him run the ranch. After Dad was killed, the foreman told me he wasn't working for a woman.

"The three men who rode in with you are the only men I have left. When my foreman quit, four of my other men left with him." Indian said, "Miss Star, I'll do everything possible to get your herd to Dodge City so you won't lose your ranch. If I'm working for you as your trail boss, you and everyone working the drive have to understand one thing on the drive. I'm the boss. No one questions how or what I do on the drive. If they do, they're fired."

He continued, "I can pick up some cowboys to help us. One thing we have to do is to have a good cook and a serviceable chuck wagon. Do you have a good cook working for you?"

"No. He was one of the men who quit when the foreman quit, saying he wasn't working for a woman. But I can cook, and we have a good chuck wagon. I can drive the wagon as well as any man. Dad taught me how to handle a team and how to be a good driver."

Indian asked, "Miss Star, I'm sure you can, but are you sure you want to go on this drive? It's a long ways to Dodge City, and traveling with a bunch of cowboys through the country we're going through is not going to be any picnic.

"Besides, you coming along on this drive may cause me lots of problems keeping you safe. Not only safe from the men we might meet up with on the trail, but the men going on the drive with us. "You understand what I'm talking about, don't you? You're a beautiful young woman, and you may be too much temptation for these lonesome cowboys to stand."

"How about you, Mr. Leader? Will I be too much of a temptation for you?"

"You're pretty tempting right here!"

"Well, that should give you a great incentive to keep me safe on the trail, don't you think?"

"Well, if you're going to be the cook on this drive, you'll have to find someone to work with you, because you'll have to go ahead of the herd to set up camp at night and have supper ready when the herd arrives.

"Can you find someone to help you, 'cause I won't send you ahead of the herd every day by yourself."

"Yes, I can. I'll get Granny Hayes to go with me. She been on lots of long drives working with her husband when he was setting up relay stations for the stage line.

"She can shoot, and she can drive a team. She's one person you can depend on to help keep the cowboys in line as far as I'm concerned. She'd shoot their eyes out.

"One other thing, from now on, it's just first names, OK, Indian?"

"That's OK with me, Serene, first names only.

"Serene, tell me about the rustlers. Have you been having trouble with them for a long time, or is this something new?"

"No, we never had any trouble with rustling until about a month ago. One of our men came upon them when they had about fifty head of our steers.

"When he tried to stop them, they shot him. He lived long enough to tell us what happened. Then we lost two other men, then my father.

"Some of the men think it's one of the local ranchers who is stealing our cattle because then we wouldn't have enough cattle left to sell to pay off our debt, and then they could buy up our land pretty cheap. We are the largest ranch in the area. We're not as big as the King Ranch, but we're pretty big."

"What do you think, Serene, could it be one of the ranchers stealing your cattle?"

"I guess it's possible, but in the past we've always had good relationships with our neighboring ranchers. So I doubt it.

"However, we do have one new neighbor who recently bought the ranch adjacent to us. He seems like a nice man. He's even asked me to a dance once at a church dance. He even proposed marriage to me once."

"Did you go with him and tell him you'd marry him?"

"Not that it's any of your business who I have a date with or who I marry, but no, I didn't go with him, and I'm sure not going to marry him.

"I have too many things I need to do to take care on this ranch. I owe it to my father to keep this ranch going after he spent almost fifty years building it."

"Good. I'm glad you didn't go on a date with him and that you're not going to marry him."

"What difference does it make to you?"

"I don't know, Serene, but somehow it seems like it makes a big difference to me. I guess I better get busy planning the cattle drive to Dodge City and quit thinking about whom you might go on a date with or who you'd marry."

"Yes, sir, Mr. Trail Boss. You better get busy with your job and quit thinking about me."

"I think that's going to be harder to do for me than I ever thought. I've never spent any time thinking about any woman before.

"If I can be excused, I'll find my way to the bunkhouse and begin figuring out how we are going to get your three thousand head of cattle to market before a blizzard gets all of us."

Serene smiled and put out her hand and took his hand and said, "Thank you, Indian. I'm really glad you're here. I sure need your help, and from what I hear, you're the only man that could do it."

"This late in the season, I'm probably the only trail boss dumb enough to try."

"Good night, Indian. Thanks again for coming to help me." "Good night, Serene. I'll see you in the morning."

Indian couldn't believe he was flirting with Serene; he never did that with any woman. He just shook his head and muttered to himself, "I can't believe it was me saying those things to her."

Indian found his way to the bunkhouse and an empty bed, which wasn't hard to do since this bunkhouse could sleep twenty men and right now there were only four men working at the Star Ranch.

Indian began making plans for the drive; the first decision he made was he had to hire more men than the normal ten to twelve men for this drive. He already determined that Teddy Smith would be the horse wrangler for this drive.

Then he decided he needed to ride back to Cuero to see if could hire some drovers right now. He didn't have any time to waste. He wanted to hire fifteen or sixteen men for this drive, and he needed at least ten more men right now to help round up the cattle before they could get started.

Indian asked Teddy, "Find me a good horse and saddle him. My horse needs rest, and I want to go to Cuero to see if I can hire some men tonight."

Since it was getting close to sundown, Teddy asked him if he meant "right now."

Indian told him, "Yeah, right now!"

Teddy helped Indian take his gear into the bunkhouse, and as he was carrying in the two extra Winchesters rifles he said, "You sure got lots of guns. You expecting a lot of trouble coming here?"

Indian replied, "No, sir, I wasn't expecting trouble. I just had trouble on the way here and ended up with some extra hardware."

Teddy grunted, "Oh, I understand."

Teddy didn't really understand at all, but he wasn't going to press the issue with Indian.

He already found that Indian could take care of himself, as he remembered his sore neck from Indian's boot holding him on the ground earlier in the day.

Teddy went to the corral and picked out a good horse for Indian to ride and saddled him with Indian's saddle and his rifle. Then he brought the horse back to the bunkhouse for Indian.

Indian thanked Teddy, got on the horse, and galloped away from the bunkhouse.

About an hour later, the ranch hands headed for the cookhouse where Serene had supper ready for them.

When they came in for supper, Serene asked, "Toby, where's Mr. Leader?"

"He told Teddy he was going to Cuero to hire some drovers, Miss Star."

"Damn, I guess after I told him I was the cook, he left so he didn't have to eat the supper I fixed."

The three men laughed loudly.

Teddy said, "You're the best cook we've ever had. You're as good as my mommy!"

Indian was riding hard to cover the ten miles back to Cuero and thinking just as hard about his meeting with his new boss lady, Serene Star. He had never met anyone like her, or never saw anyone who looked like her.

Indian knew she was one smart woman. She certainly had him tied around her little finger with just one one-hour meeting. He already knew he would give his life for her if she asked him to.

Serene was the Star Ranch, and since she was the Star Ranch, the brand meant more to him than any ranch he had ever worked for. OK, the fact was she meant more to him than anyone he ever worked for, and that was saying a lot, because he had worked for a lot of good men.

Maybe that was the key; they were all men, and Serene was a woman and what a woman!

He loved her name and said it over and over, "Serene, Serene, Serene!" What a beautiful name. He loved it.

CHAPTER THREE

HIRING DROVERS IN CUERO, TEXAS

NDIAN ARRIVED IN CUERO at about nine o'clock that night and headed directly to the only saloon he saw. Besides, it was the only place in town that was open that late at night.

He got off his horse and was careful as he headed for the swinging doors of the saloon. He remembered the last time he approached a saloon when some stupid kid came flying out the door trying to kill him.

This time no one came out the swinging doors yelling, "I hate the way you look." He didn't even have to kill anybody to get into the saloon.

Arriving inside the saloon, Indian saw only four people sitting at a table playing poker. No one looked up at him when he came in; they were busy with their card game.

The bartender was sitting at the end of the bar reading a book. When he saw Indian, he slowly put down his book and asked if he could help him.

"Whiskey."

The bartender got up from his stool and picked up a bottle and a shot glass and poured Indian a drink.

Indian said, "I'm looking for some drovers to take a herd of cattle up to Dodge City. Do you know where I can find some good men?"

"This time of year I think you could probably take your pick unless they're afraid to go on a trail drive this late in the year."

The bartender yelled over to the men playing poker and asked, "You men interested in going on a trail drive this time of year?"

One of the men got up from the table, folded his cards, and said to his fellow players, "Count me out of this hand."

The man walked over to the bar where Indian and the bartender were.

He asked, "Who's looking for drovers this time of the year?" Indian replied, "The Star Ranch."

The man said, "Nope. I don't think so. They got bad problems. They're jinxed."

Indian said, "They're not jinxed. They've just run into a lot of bad luck right now."

The man said, "Well, if that's their problem, then it's a really a bad spell of bad luck. I got enough problems of my own without taking on theirs.

"One more question before I go back to my game, who's their trail boss for the drive?"

"I am." Indian replied. "And who might you be?"

"I'm Indian Leader. I'm the trail boss for the drive."

"Well, that does make a big difference. I've heard a lot of good things about you, and the things I've heard tells me I'd ride with you. So, by God, I'll go with you.

"Mr. Leader, I'm Alex Gonzales. I'm sure I can get you some more drovers if you need them."

Indian stuck out his hand and shook hands with Alex and replied, "I sure need about fourteen more good men for this drive."

"Well, I can't get you fourteen from my family, but I can get you my brothers and cousins. There's Enquire, Flex, Mark, Michael, they're all Gonzales."

"Great start, how many of them have experience taking a herd to Dodge City?"

"I'm the only one who's been on that drive, but the others have been on drives to Abilene and to some other places, some of them more than once."

"That's good, because taking a herd this time of the year may be a tough job because of the weather."

"Well, if you weren't the trail boss on this drive, I wouldn't be going. I'm sure the other members of my family wouldn't either."

"Thanks, Alex. You're going to be one of my point men for this drive."

That pleased Alex very much since he had never got to ride point before.

Alex replied, "Thanks, Boss. I'll do a good job for you." "I'm sure you will, or you wouldn't be getting the job."

The other three men at the table had been listening to the conversation between Indian and Alex, and they got up from the card table and approached Indian and said they would go on the drive.

One of the men was Miguel Cabrera, and he said he had friends who would go on the drive and all of them had experience on trail drives. He told Indian he would get Willard and Michael Chrisman; Adam and Arthur Davis; and Carlos Espinal.

The next man name was Alejandra Gonzalez, and he could bring along his brother, Juan. He said they had made a couple of drives last year.

The third man's name was Ephraim Espinoza, and he would get his friend Rodriguez Espinosa to go on the drive with him. They had been on two drives already this year.

Indian shook hands with each of the men, bought them a drink, and said, "Here's the deal: you will all be getting forty dollars a month, and if we don't lose more than a hundred head of cattle, you'll get a bonus of forty dollars.

"I expect all of you to be at the Star Ranch day after tomorrow and be ready to go to work rounding up cattle so we can get this drive started.

"I don't have any idea how long this drive is going to take, but the sooner we get started on the drive, the better chance we have making the drive without getting into a blizzard somewhere along the trail.

"Good night, gentlemen. I look forward seeing you and the other men you said you could bring early in the morning, day after tomorrow at the Star Ranch."

Indian left the saloon and mounted his horse and headed back in the direction of the Star Ranch. It had been a long day, and he needed some sleep.

He slept in the saddle as he rode back to the ranch; once in a while he would wake up to be sure they were still moving along in the general direction of the ranch.

About the time the sun was coming up, he saw he was almost at the Star Ranch headquarters. Teddy had picked him out a good horse, one that knew his way home.

Indian dismounted his horse and went inside the bunkhouse where the men were just getting up for the day.

He asked Teddy to unsaddle his horse after he got dressed and to give his horse some extra grain, 'cause he had a long night.

Indian lay down on his bunk and stayed there for about an hour. He got up and tried to clean himself up and shave, but he was so tried he didn't do a very good job of either.

The other three men had already gone over to the cookhouse for breakfast by the time Indian got up.

Indian sure needed a cup of coffee after his long night ride. He was pleased to see Serene standing in the cookhouse with her apron on, pouring coffee for the men sitting at the table when he got there.

Indian said, "Good morning, Miss Serene. How are you this morning?"

She took one look at Indian and said, "It looks like I'm in a lot better shape this morning then you are, cowboy."

"Yes, ma'am, I reckon you are, but I could sure use some of that coffee you're pouring."

"You've got it, cowboy." She handed him a cup of hot coffee. Indian drank down the coffee in one gulp and asked for more. Serene said, "You must have had a big night in town, cowboy."

"Yes, ma'am. I hired us fourteen drovers that will be here tomorrow morning to start rounding up the herd so we can get moving.

"We can't drive cattle until we get them rounded up."

"Well, that's not the kind of night I thought you had in town. That's for sure."

"Ma'am, I'm working for you and am going to keep working for you until we get three thousand head of your cattle to Dodge City, Kansas.

"If we're lucky that's going to take us about a hundred days. "After we do that, then I'll take a day or two off. But right now, every day we're delayed getting started puts us in more danger getting caught in a blizzard. That's not where any of us want to be." Serene asked, "Indian, would you like some breakfast before you start doing anything else?"

"Yes, ma'am. I would like about four eggs and about a pound of bacon and a loaf of bread and some butter if you got some."

"Sit down and have another cup or two of coffee. I'll see what I can do."

She sat the coffee pot down in front of him.

"I'm sorry, ma'am, about wanting so much to eat for breakfast, but I guess I plum forgot about getting something to eat yesterday." Serene replied, "Don't worry. I'll get you something to eat as soon as I can."

Indian sat down at the table and finished three more cups of coffee while he talked to Teddy, Toby, and Lloyd about which two of them would be staying and looking after the ranch while Miss Star was gone.

Teddy said, "Indian, it has to be Toby and Lloyd, because you already told me I could be the horse wrangler on the drive."

"That's right. I did tell you that, but at the time I was thinking all three of you would be going on the drive, but we can't leave the ranch without someone to look after the rest of the stock."

Lloyd replied, "I'm happy to stay here and look after things. I been on those drives, and it's a tough job."

Toby chimed in, "Me, too. I got a new gal, and I don't want her taken away from me by some other cowboy while I'm gone for four or five months."

Indian said, "Well, I guess that settles that. One other thing we probably need to do is to find a couple more hands to help look after the ranch while everybody else is gone. Do any of you know somebody who needs a job?"

Lloyd replied, "I heard Del and Bob Webb returned from Wyoming a month or so ago, and they're looking for work."

Indian said, "We should talk to Miss Serene about them to see if she knows them, and if she thought they would be OK to be working on the ranch."

Serene returned from the kitchen carrying a large platter and set it down in front of Indian and said, "OK, cowboy, let's see you eat every bite on that platter."

"It looks great, Miss Serene. I'm going to do my best to eat it all."

Serene sat down directly across from Indian and watched as he ate every morsel of food on the platter.

She smiled at him and said, "I guess you don't think my cooking is so bad after all. I thought you went to town to keep from eating my dinner last night."

"You'd be dead wrong about that. That's the best meal I've had in years. If you do as well on the trail as you did in this kitchen, we're going to have the best-fed drovers on the trail and maybe the fattest ones, too."

Everyone laughed at that.

Indian said, "Miss Serene, I need to speak with you about several things when you have time."

"OK, Indian, let's go to my office. I'll take care of these dishes after a while."

CHAPTER FOUR

BUSINESS MEETING WITH THE BOSS LADY

NDIAN SPOKE FIRST. "SERENE, here's what I promised the drovers I hired last night. They would be paid forty dollars a month, and if we didn't lose more than a hundred head of cattle on the trip, they would get a bonus of forty dollars.

"I told them to report here tomorrow so we could get busy rounding up the cattle so we can get started as soon as possible. They claim all of the drovers coming tomorrow have trail experience. I don't know if that's true or not, but once I work with them, it won't take me long to find out. And if they haven't had the experience, they will soon learn."

Serene said, "I don't see any problem with the arrangement you made with them. It sounds fair to me."

"Serene, I also talked to Teddy, Toby, and Lloyd about a couple of them staying here on the ranch while we're gone, and Toby and Lloyd said they would like to stay.

"I also told them they probably would need a couple more hands to help while we're gone, and Lloyd said Del and Bob Webb recently returned from Wyoming and they were looking for work. Do you know them?"

"Indian, I never thought about having someone here to look after the ranch and the rest of the herd while we are gone, but that's right. We've got to have people working here while we're gone.

"I don't know the Webb Boys, but if Lloyd suggested them, I think they would be all right."

"What kind of a worker is Lloyd, and how long has he worked for the ranch?"

"Dad always said he was a good man and knew a lot about cattle, and I agree. He's worked here for five years."

"If you don't have someone else in mind, you might consider promoting him to foreman or at least putting him in charge while you're gone and see how he does. Then if he does well, you could make him your foreman."

"That's a great idea."

"Serene, I'd bring him in here and tell him that while you're gone, he's going to be in charge of the ranch and tell him you'll pay him another ten dollars a month."

"Thanks, Indian. I'll do it, and I'll let him hire the Webb Boys himself."

"Serene, one more thing. We didn't discuss what I get paid to be your trail boss. I get one hundred and twenty-five dollars a month and a bonus at the end of the drive."

"How much bonus?"

"I'll leave that to you after we see how well we do selling the herd. Before we leave, I think I will contact some of the buyers I know and see if we couldn't get a little more money for each head of cattle, since we'll be about the only herd coming in this time of the year.

"I'm thinking it might be possible to get a little extra for each steer we bring to them so late in the season."

"That's a great idea, Indian. I don't know what I would do without you guiding me on this drive."

"Serene, I'm sure you could've gotten someone to help you, but I'm glad it's me.

"I'm going to take a ride around the ranch to see how long it's going to take us to round the cattle up before we can leave."

"Indian, you should take Lloyd with you so you know when you are on my ranch."

"Thanks. That's a good idea."

Indian and Serene got up from their chairs, and when she came around the desk, she put her hand on his. Indian took her hand and held it to his lips and gently kissed it and said, "I'm so happy to be working for you."

He released her hand, and she retorted, "Bet you say that to everybody you work for."

"I've never kissed their hand before."

Indian quickly turned and walked out the door.

He wondered, "Why did I do that? What made me do it?" He had more questions than answers; he had never thought about taking a woman's hand before and kissing it, but he just did.

Maybe Serene was right; maybe she was too much of a temptation for him to spend four or five months on the trail with.

Before he was worried about her being too much of a temptation for the cowboys on the drive; now he was worried about her being too much of a temptation for him.

What did she think about him now? He was noted for being the ultimate professional trail boss, not some woman-grabbing cowboy.

After Indian left her office, Serene sat back down and tried to think about what had just happened. She remembered her hand touching Indian's hand; then he took her hand and softly kissed it, and then he rushed out of her office.

She wasn't sure why she felt so excited; it was just a kiss on the hand, for goodness' sake, but it was his lips on her hand.

She said out loud to herself, "Serene, you're falling for this cowboy? My God, a long time ago my mommy told me about cowboys.

"Mommy said, 'Never fall for a cowboy. They'll break your heart, leave you alone, and they never stay in one place.'"

Back east when she was going to school, she'd had several dates with boys, but none of them ever meant anything to her. They were fun to be with, but she knew they would never leave the big cities in the east to live on a ranch in Texas like she planned to do. So they were just fun to be with, and she was never serious about them.

She was truly her daddy's girl; she wanted to live and work the ranch for as long as she lived, and nothing else would do. Right now she had a problem to solve, and she really needed Indian to get her herd to Dodge so she could sell them and pay off the bank loan.

Serene was truly confused. Was Indian the shining knight on the white horse sent to save her, like she'd read about in books, or was he just another cowboy?

One like her mother always warned her about, "They'll love you, and then leave you." Was Indian like that?

Hell, she didn't know how she felt about him. How was she to know what he felt about her?

Indian asked Lloyd to ride around the ranch with him to see how many steers they could find and where they were.

Lloyd told Indian he would saddle up a couple of horses, and they could take a ride around some of the ranch that was close to ranch headquarters.

As they were riding away from the ranch headquarters, Indian said to Lloyd, "How many acres is the Star Ranch?"

"I'm not really sure, but with the new section of property Mr. Star bought last year, I'd say about twenty-five thousand acres, give or take a few hundred acres."

"That's a lot ranch, Lloyd."

"Sure is, and it's hard to keep up with the cattle with that much land."

"Lloyd, do you have line camps on the ranch for cowboys to work from?"

"Yeah, we have three of them. But since we already sent six thousand head to market this year, we don't need them, and we don't have the men to work them anyway."

As they rode around areas close to the main ranch headquarters, they found a lot of cattle. Indian wasn't sure how many they saw, but he thought it might be easier to round up three thousand head then he had assumed.

Lloyd told him because of the rustlers they had been driving the cattle closer to ranch headquarters. Mr. Star knew Indian was coming soon, and he wanted him to be able to get started on the drive as soon as possible.

"I'm sure glad to see what I'm seeing and appreciate the effort Mr. Star and you folks did to help us get started on the drive." "Yeah, Mr. Star was a good man and a great cowman. I was so sorry to see him gunned down like that."

Indian and Lloyd rode back to the ranch headquarters without anything else being said.

Later that day, Indian rode the ten miles back to Cuero to send telegraphs to the cattle buyers he knew in Dodge to see what they might be willing to pay for a herd this late in the year.

While Indian was in town he stopped at the local saloon to thank the bartender for his help in getting him some men to work the trail drive for him.

Since he was there, he decided he could have a shot of whiskey before he went back to the ranch.

During his visit to the saloon, a tall, well-dressed man came into the saloon and took a seat at one of the tables and asked the bartender to bring him a bottle.

Indian thought the man looked familiar, but he wasn't sure where he had seen him before. Indian didn't say anything to the man since he wasn't sure if he knew him or not. Something told him he knew this man, but he sure couldn't place him.

CHAPTER FIVE

SEPTEMBER ROUNDUP AT STAR RANCH

THE NEXT MORNING ALL the drovers about whom Indian had been told showed up as promised. "Great start," Indian thought!

While the men were still on their horses, Indian asked Serene to come out so he could introduce her to the men, and at the same time, he said he would tell the men what he expected from his drovers. Serene and Indian went out to meet the new men.

Indian said, "My name is Indian Leader, and I'm the trail boss on the drive to Dodge City.

"Gentlemen, at this time I want to introduce you to Miss Serene Star, the owner of Star Ranch, and she's our boss lady. You will be seeing a lot of her on this drive because she and Granny Hayes will be doing the cooking on this drive.

"I can't tell you if she's a better cook than any of the other trail cooks you had, but I'm sure it's safe to say she the best-looking cook you ever had. One thing to remember, she may be our cook, but she still is the boss of this outfit.

"Because she and Granny Hayes will be on this drive, I want all of you to watch your language around the chuck wagon. In other words, on this drive you will be acting like you're going to church. "If you have trouble remembering how it was going to church, I'll be happy to help your memory.

"I run a tight outfit, but a fair one. No one makes decisions on this drive but me. Sometimes you may not like my decisions, but once you sign on for this drive, what I say goes.

"I do things a little differently from most trail bosses. All of you will be rotated around the herd except my two point men, who, on this drive, are Alex Gonzales and Miguel Cabrera. Every man gets his chance to work drag on this drive and all the other positions on the drive except the two point men.

"Nobody likes working drag, but we still have to have people there to move the herd and not lose stragglers along the way. It's as important as any other position on the drive. Also, I don't allow whiskey on the drive. The only whiskey allowed is what the cook has to use as medicine.

"One thing I'm very proud to say is I never lost a herd, and I've never lost a man when I was the trail boss. Just so you know it, I'm not planning on losing any of you or losing this herd. We may have a hard time on this drive because it's so late in the year, but with a little luck, maybe, just maybe, we'll make it without getting into a blizzard. If we don't, we're still going to make it to Dodge with every cow that can walk and every cowboy we left home with.

"When you ride for me, I ride for you. I'll never leave a man behind. I know I've talked enough, but I want a clear understanding of what's expected of you and what you can expect from me on this drive before you sign up.

"I'll be helping Miss Serene write each of your names on the payroll ledger that's going with us to Dodge. Anybody that doesn't want to go with us can leave now without any hard feelings."

Serene took out a payroll ledger to record each man's name as they came up to her desk; she had had her desk moved outside for this purpose. Every man there came forward and gave Serene their name. They were as follows:

Alex Gonzales, Enrique Gonzales, Felix Gonzales, Mark Gonzales, Michael Gonzales, Alejandra Gonzalez, Juan Gonzalez, Ephraim Espinoza, Carlos Espinal, Adam Davis, Arthur Davis, Willard Chrisman, Michael Chrisman, Miguel Cabrera, and Rodriguez Espinosa.

After Serene wrote each of the men's names down in the ledger, she thanked them for coming to help her.

Indian then directed Teddy to take five men and go to one area of the ranch to start gathering up all the cattle they could find and bring them to a large area close to the ranch headquarters.

Indian told Toby and Lloyd to do the same thing; each was to take five men and go to other areas of the ranch and bring in as many cows as they could find and merge them all together into one large herd.

After everyone left the ranch headquarters to round up cattle to make up the herd, Serene said to Indian, "You sure did a good job in a hurry getting things started."

"Thanks, Serene, but I'm just doing my job." "So far you are doing your job very well."

"You don't have to thank me for doing my job. You can thank me when we turn the herd over to a buyer in Dodge.

One thing, Serene, you need to get Granny Hayes here to help list the supplies you're going to need on the trail and get the chuck wagon loaded as soon as you can. I don't want to have to wait on you when the herd is ready to move."

"You don't have to worry about us being ready, Mr. Trail Boss. We will be ready to go in two days."

"Great, I'm going to head out to see how the men are doing rounding up the cattle."

"Good. I'll see you and the rest of the men at supper time." Indian thought she sounded kind of mad at him the way she said it. He guessed she would either get over her mad or she wouldn't. Right now he didn't care one way or the other. He had lots of work to do.

Before he could get away from the ranch headquarters, ten riders showed up.

One of them said, "We're looking for Indian Leader." "I'm him. What can I do for you?"

"We heard in town you were looking for drovers, and we're looking for work and wanted to know if you could use more men."

"How many of you have trail-driving experience?" Several of the men shouted, "I have."

Indian said, "I want to see a show of hands of you men that have had experience on a trail drive."

Six of the men raised their hands.

Indian said, "I'll take all of you that have had experience if you are willing to work as wranglers for thirty dollars a month, and if we don't lose more than a hundred head of cattle, you'll each get a bonus of forty dollars at the end of the drive. How many of you want to go on these conditions?"

Indian was surprised when all of them said they would go on the drive.

Indian said, "OK, gentlemen. I'll get the boss lady and get you signed up for the drive.

"You other four men wait till we get the men going on the drive signed up, and I'll see if you might be interested in working on the ranch."

Indian went to the ranch house and knocked on the door; when Serene came to the door she was surprised to see Indian standing there.

She said, "You lost, cowboy?"

"Nope. We just got six more men to go with us on the drive to help take care of the horses, and we need to sign them up on the payroll."

"You sure we need six more men to take care of the horses?" "Yeah, we do."

"OK, then I'll get the payroll ledger and meet you at the desk." "One more thing, Serene. Are you mad at me?"

"Why? Should I be?"

"I don't know. It was just the way you talked to me a while ago."

"Forget it, cowboy. If I was, I'm over it now."

"Good. Serene, I got four more men looking for work waiting over by the desk, and I said I'd see if we could use them on the ranch. I don't think five men will be enough to look after the ranch while we're gone for four or five months. What do you think?"

"I think if you keep hiring people, we'll need another herd to sell to pay the payroll. However, I think you're right. We could use them."

"OK. I'll see you at your desk."

Indian turned and started walking back to the desk to help Serene sign up the new men, when two of the men who had said they wanted to go on the drive suddenly stepped away from the other men.

One of the two men said, "OK, Indian, you've made your last trail drive," and both men reached for their guns.

Instantly, Indian dropped to the ground and pulled his gun and fired at the man who had threatened him. The man got a shot off that went over Indian's head. The man fell to the ground, and Indian rolled over and took aim at the second man and fired his Colt before the second man could get his gun aimed at him.

The first man Indian shot was lying on the ground and was trying to reach for his gun lying next to him. When Indian saw him reaching to get his gun, he put a shot through his head; he wouldn't be reaching for anything ever again.

The second man Indian had shot fell straight down on his face and never moved. Indian still approached him cautiously. The man never moved, and his gun was lying under him. Indian reached down and slowly turned him over on his back.

He was dead all right; he had shot him right between the eyes.

Indian then turned to the other men who had come with these two men with his six-guns still in his hand, pointing in their direction, checking to see if any of them might be trying to kill him.

He quickly saw the other men were standing there in shock. Indian put his Colt in his holster and asked, "Does anybody here know these men?"

One of the young men who didn't have trail experience said, "I don't know their names, but I know that they used to work for Kent Eagle at The Double Eagle Ranch. I thought they still worked for him, but they said they needed a job and came from town with the rest of us."

Indian still kept his hand on his gun and asked, "Do any of you men work for the Double Eagle Ranch?"

The universal answer from the rest of the men was "No, sir!" Serene had come out on the porch just when the trouble started and saw the gunfight. She was afraid those two men would kill Indian, and her ranch would be lost. Thank God, he was alive. Suddenly it occurred to her that she was more afraid of losing Indian than she was of losing the ranch.

Damn cowboy! She thought, "Damn, I am falling in love with him."

Serene rushed to Indian and asked, "Are you OK, Indian?"

"I'm OK, but I think I might have to have a talk with Mr. Kent Eagle to see what he knows about this."

"Please don't. Something might happen to you, and I can't afford to lose you."

Indian said, "OK, Serene, we'll talk about this later. Right now, let's get these men signed on the payroll ledger."

Serene took her place behind her desk.

Indian asked, "If two more of you men want to make the drive, let me know now, and we'll sign you up. Two men raised their hands. So Indian began getting the names of the men going on the drive with them. Their names were Keith Easterday, Dan Dyer, Ed Williams, Chuck Autumn, Randy Call, and Steve Scott.

Indian asked the other two men if they would like to stay at the ranch and work there.

Both men said they wanted the jobs; they were Jim Reaves and Roy Bacon.

After all the men's names had been put in the payroll ledger, Indian told all the men going on the drive to take their horses and head out on the ranch; they would find three crews rounding up cattle. "Two of you join up with each crew."

Indian said, "Jim, Roy, I want you to take any valuables these men had on them and put them in the bunkhouse. Unsaddle their horses and put them in the corral, and ask Miss Serene where you can bury these men."

Roy asked, "What do you want us to do with their saddles?"

"Put them in the barn."

Roy responded, "OK, Boss, we'll get it done."

Before Indian left to go out to see how the roundup was going, he went into the bunkhouse and opened his saddlebag and dug deep down into the bottom of the bag and took out a canvas bag.

He opened the bag and took out a specially made holster he had designed to hold another pistol on the left side of his gun belt. This holster was designed to tilt the butt of the gun's handle to a position where he could easily draw it with his right hand.

When he was serving as a deputy sheriff, he found sometimes one gun wasn't enough, and this design made it easier for him to draw when he was on his horse or sitting down.

Indian said to himself, "Damn, I might as well have stayed a deputy. Killing five men in less than a month. I never had to kill that many men in a month when I was a deputy. Hell, when I was a deputy, I never killed that many men in two years."

The problem Indian now had in his head was he thought this was just the beginning of the killings. On one hand he had the Phillips to worry about, and now it looked like he had the Double Eagle people to worry about too.

Indian hooked the other holster on his gun belt and then put the other gun he had in the canvas bag in the holster. He thought,

"Now I only need my badge to be right back to where I never wanted to be, a target for every gunslinger in the west."

Indian took the bullets out of his gun belt and replaced the three spent shells in his Colt. He was ready again in case he had more trouble today.

Indian now remembered who the tall, dark, well-dressed man was he saw in the saloon. It was Kent Eagle; only, when he knew him back in St. Louis County, Missouri, he went by the name of Black Jack Eagle—a professional gambler and hired gun. Yeah, Indian knew him all right.

He'd had several run-ins with him when he was a deputy in St. Louis County. The only thing was Black Jack always had enough witnesses to say the other fellow drew first, so they could never make anything stick on him, nor could they do anything about him.

One thing Indian knew for sure was Black Jack was fast on the draw and didn't have any problem about who he shot and killed. Yes, Black Jack would be the man who would be behind rustling cattle and asking Serene to marry him to get control of her ranch; besides, she would make a nice trophy wife as well.

Indian had never liked him before, and now he had a really good reason to hate him!

Right now though, Black Jack Eagle would have to wait his turn; first, Indian had to get the Star Ranch's cattle to Dodge City.

CHAPTER SIX

LET THE DRIVE BEGIN

NDIAN WAS SURPRISED AND pleased that it took his crew only a week to gather up three thousand head of Longhorn steers, and they were ready to start for Dodge.

Serene did her part too; she and Granny Hayes had the chuck wagon loaded with supplies, and they were ready to leave in two days, just like she said she would be.

Indian told her she did a great job.

Granny Hayes was Teddy's grandmother; her daughter was Teddy's mother, so he had a family member traveling with him on his first great adventure out of DeWitt County.

Indian thought Granny Hayes was everything Serene said she was: she could drive a team very well, she certainly knew what they needed in the way of food for the trail, she could sew, and she knew a lot about medicine.

He hadn't seen her shoot, but she carried her Winchester rifle like it was an old friend. So he was guessing she would be able to hold her own with it.

Indian had the men riding night herd every night after they started gathering the herd. He was concerned rustlers would try to take the herd after they had the cattle rounded up. He was happy no one tried to take the herd or stampede it before they even got off the ranch.

His other worry was that whoever was trying to get Star Ranch wouldn't miss a chance to disrupt their plans with every step of the drive, and he wasn't sure they wouldn't still try something before the herd started moving north.

Now they had started; the herd began moving and would soon be strung out over several miles. Driving Longhorns was different from moving other cattle. They just kind of strung out in long lines with natural leaders taking their place at the front on the herd with others following them in an irregular line behind them.

They had their own way of moving; you couldn't lead them and you couldn't crowd them too close on the sides, or they'd bolt and run away from the herd.

Soon several natural leaders moved to the front of the herd, and the rest of the cattle followed in behind them. The drovers rode in pairs on each side of the herd using hand signals to communicate with each other. Alex Gonzales and Miguel Cabrera were riding point and guiding the cattle in the general direction they wanted the herd to go.

The herd was moving toward Bandera, Texas, which was northwest of San Antonio by several miles. There they would pick up the Great Western Trail and continue north on the trail for about four hundred fifty miles to cross the Red River into Indian Territory.

Indian received a reply from two of the three cattle buyers in Dodge before they left on the drive, giving him a price they would pay for the herd. He was told if they could get the herd to Dodge by December 10, both buyers offered him thirty to thirty-five dollars a head.

They had thirteen weeks to get to Dodge to make that date. Indian calculated that they would need to average about eighteen miles a day, which were a few more miles than Indian liked to average, but maybe it was possible.

Serene was thrilled to hear what they were offered for each head of cattle.

Indian said, "Don't count your money yet. We've got a long way to go before we get there, and a lot can happen between here and Dodge."

Serene said, "I know that, but I also know you will get us there."

"Glad you think so."

"I don't think so. I know so!"

Indian rode ahead of the herd, looking for someplace to camp for the night. Serene and Granny Hayes, driving the chuck wagon, were following in the same general direction Indian had taken.

Three hours later, Serene saw Indian riding toward them, and she stopped the chuck wagon to wait for him. Seeing Indian, Serene started smiling and waving to him.

Granny Hayes said, "Child, I think you got a thing for the trail boss man, don't you?"

"Granny, I think I do, but I don't know for sure. How do you know if you love someone, Granny?"

"You'll know, child."

By that time, Indian arrived at the chuck wagon and told Serene, "I picked you out a nice place on the Cibolo Creek to set up camp for the night. It's about five miles ahead of you. There're several large trees where you can set up the chuck wagon, and there's plenty of wide open space along the creek for the cattle to spend the night.

"I'm headed back to the herd to help guide them to our campsite. Adios. I'll see you later this evening."

He gave them a big smile as he rode away at a gallop.

It was about two hours before Indian could see the herd coming. When he got closer to the herd, he made a wide swing around the lead animals so he didn't cause a stampede.

When he was well behind Alex, he slowly turned his horse around and walked his horse up next to Alex.

He told Alex they had about three hours of riding before they got to the site to bed down for the night; they had been traveling for almost nine hours already.

Indian knew there were going to be some tired and sore cowboys tonight after spending twelve hours in the saddle, and they still had to ride night herd and start it all over again in the morning.

Indian was hoping they could get a long ways from Cuero before Black Jack Eagle knew they left. He didn't want to fight with him and his men out here on the open range, and at the same time, he wanted to keep the herd from stampeding.

As Indian was worrying about Black Jack Eagle, Serene was worrying about her feelings about Indian.

She had spent a lot of her years growing up in the east and getting her education there. She wasn't sure she was really ready to fall in love, and she wasn't sure Indian really had that much interest in her.

She learned about a lot of things in the east, but she was perhaps lacking a lot of knowledge about human relationships. She knew how to do bookkeeping and how to write proper business letters; she knew a lot about law, and she even learned how to use one of those new sewing machines; she even bought one and brought it to Texas with her when she came home. It was probably the first sewing machine in Texas, and she'd made lots of clothes on it already.

Serene was still in contact with her friends in Boston; Washington, DC; and New York City. Several of her old friends kept trying to get her to come back and live in the east.

Her teachers encouraged her to stay and teach or to go into teaching when she returned to Texas. But Serene's heart was in ranching; she loved everything about it, and it was all she ever wanted to do.

Maybe someday she would like to have a husband and children to share her life with her, but until Indian came into her life, she never spent much time thinking about it. Now it seemed like that was all she could think about.

Indian moved away from the herd, and after he was a safe distance away, he pushed his horse into a gallop and headed straight for the campsite he had selected earlier.

He slowed down his horse as he came up to the chuck wagon and saw that the team had been unhitched and hobbled so they couldn't get far away from the campsite. He saw there was a nice fire going, and Serene and Granny were busy preparing the evening meal.

He stepped down from his horse and dropped the reins to the ground and walked over to say "hi" to Serene and Granny. They both stopped what they were doing and gave him a smile.

Indian said, "Looks like you two are doing OK, working on the evening meal. I know a bunch of tired, hungry cowboys that are going to be really happy to get off their horses and get something to eat after their first day on the trail."

Granny replied, "We'll be ready for them when they get here." "That's good. How are you holding out, Serene?"

She smiled and replied, "It's just like I'm having a picnic in Central Park in New York City."

Indian didn't really know what Central Park was, but he said, "That's good."

He asked if there was anything he could do to help them. Serene snapped back, "You can help us the same way you would help any of your other trail cooks."

Indian was surprised by her remark but answered, "Right! In other words, the answer is no, you don't need my help."

Granny said, "You've got that right, cowboy. We'll do our job. You just see to yours."

"Yes, ma'am."

After that exchange of words Indian got back on his horse and rode back toward the herd as the lead steers were beginning to be turned in a circle around Alex.

The drovers keep working the lead group of the herd around in a circle until all the steers in the lead group came to a stop and some began drinking from the creek and others began chewing on the grass.

When the other groups arrived where the first group had stopped, they stopped too. This process took a long time since the herd was strung out for probably two or three miles behind the leaders.

Indian told the drovers from the lead group to head over to the chuck wagon to get something to eat because they would be the first of the night riders to look after the herd when the entire herd had stopped for the night.

Indian told Alex and Miguel that they needed to have men on both sides of the creek to be sure the herd didn't wander away during the night, and he wanted four men on each shift for the next few nights.

He told them he was afraid those rustlers might try grabbing the herd before they got too far away from Cuero. They understood what he meant.

Each of the night crews would work in two-hour shifts all night long.

Teddy, Dan, and Ed Williams, the three horse wranglers, arrived with the spare horses at the campsite after most of the cowboys had already had their meal.

Granny Hayes was glad to see her grandson, Teddy, who was still smiling and happy after his first day on the long trip to Kansas.

The wranglers had had a busy day learning which string of horses was assigned to each drover and changing out horses for each of them.

During the drive to Dodge City, each drover on this drive had ten horses assigned to him. They had a total of two hundred and twenty head of horses in the remuda—that's the name given to the herd of spare horses.

Every day of the drive, each cowboy would change horses three to four times a day, and it was the only time during his ten to twelve hours day he was off his horse.

One of the three wranglers would take a horse from a drover's string of horses up to him and exchange his tired mount for a fresh one. The drover was only off his horse long enough to remove his saddle and bridle and re-saddle and re-bridle his fresh mount.

Then he was back on his horse and back in his position on the drive assigned to him that day. Normally, the position on a trail drive the drover is assigned is the same position every day, based on his knowledge and experience.

While working a trail drive with Indian Leader, things were not done in a normal way. Every cowboy, except the point men, would be working the drag position; it was the dirtiest job on the drive trailing behind the herd.

You were eating dirt all day long, not what the more experienced drovers expected to be doing on the drive.

The only thing the drovers could figure out was Indian wanted every drover to learn how to work every position on the drive.

The way they had it figured out was Indian wanted to be sure every drover could take over any position on the drive in case they had to.

All of them knew Alex and Miguel had by far the most experience working trail drives, and you needed the most experienced drovers in the point positions.

They had all the responsibility to turn the herd if they had a stampede and also to keep the Longhorns moving somewhere near the direction they were going. Sometimes this wasn't easy to do since Longhorns had their own idea about everything and where they wanted to go.

Most of the crew would almost rather work drag than have those responsibilities.

As a rule, cowboys didn't care much about taking on responsibilities.

It took a little over a week to get to Bandera, Texas, and reach the Great Western Trail. Indian thought they should have done a little bit better, but overall, he was pleased with his crew and how well Serene and Granny Hayes were doing.

CHAPTER SEVEN

NORTH UP THE GREAT WESTERN TRAIL

INDIAN DECIDED THAT NOW there was less chance of the rustlers from DeWitt County coming after the herd since they had reached the Great Western Trail.

He decided to reduce the number of night riders from four men on the two-hour shifts to two men a shift. This way, all his drovers would be able to get several more hours of sleep at night. Indian thought they would all need it.

So far, the weather had stayed warm, but the farther north they traveled, Indian felt it was getting cooler every night.

Their next landmark would be Fort Griffin; Indian knew it would take them about four weeks to get there.

One problem Indian knew they would have to face on this portion of the trip would be Indians, usually Comanche. He had dealt with them for several years now and normally didn't have much trouble with them.

He was able to talk with them and negotiate a deal with them for safe passage through their lands. He would always give them a few steers, never as many as they asked for, but enough for them to be satisfied.

The trail bosses who had the big problems with the Indians were the ones who refused to pay them a few steers for passage through their lands. When a trail boss refused to pay the Indians to cross their land, then sometime later, the Indians would come back during the night and either take several more steers than they 42 had asked for, or worse, cause the cattle to stampede and take a lot of them.

Indian understood very well the plight of the Indians. The white man wanted him to stay in one place, and the Indians didn't want to stay only on land the white man didn't want.

As Indian rode his turn at night watch, he thought back over his life, about what he had lived through and how it had made him the person he became. Like every person, he had a lot of people who had contributed to the kind of person he became.

Indian's own parents had been killed by Indians when he was five or six years old. Several days later, a very hungry, cold, and confused child was wandering around in the middle of nowhere when a small band of Cherokee Indians found him.

One Cherokee man, Charlie Whitebird, took him home, and along with his wife Moonlight, he raised Indian as their only child; he lived with them until he was fourteen years old. The only thing he had that belonged to his birth parents was a family Bible, which he was carrying when the Cherokee Indians found him.

He kept in contact with his Indian parents and visited them at least once a year. They lived in a small house in the hills in the eastern part of Indian Territory. His adopted mother still made buckskin clothes for him every time he came home to see them. They loved him like he was their own child, and he loved them.

They took very good care of him as he was growing up. They made sure he learned to read and write by taking him to the Indian mission school. At the mission school he learned about Jesus Christ and became a true believer and he still carried his family Bible with him always. When he went to bed every night, he said his prayers and was sure Jesus was looking over him.

Yeah, he thought he understood the Indians pretty well. He learned there were bad Indians, like the ones who killed his folks, and there were good Indians, like the ones who took him in and raised him as their own son. The Indians weren't any different from white men; some were bad and some were good.

After leaving his Indian parents' home, he worked for lots of different ranches, doing everything he had to do to learn to be a good cowman. He also developed a very fast draw. When he wasn't working cattle, he practiced his draw.

He drifted around the country going to new places and seeing new sites. He decided to make a trip to St. Louis because he had heard so much about the mighty Mississippi River, and he wanted to see the steamboats that traveled the river.

One night while he was in St. Louis, he was by the river watching as a steamboat was docking, when he saw a couple of men hiding in some bushes along the riverbank.

The sheriff, who was patrolling the river area, came walking by the bushes where the two men were hiding. As the sheriff passed them, they jumped out from the bushes behind the sheriff with their guns pointed at his back.

One of the men said, "Well, Sheriff Jackson, it looks like we are going to get the last laugh on you. Turn around so you can see what you've got coming."

Hearing this, Indian rushed up behind the two men, pulled his gun, and pointed it at them. Calmly he said, "You've got one chance to put your guns down on the walk, or you're both dead."

They put their guns down as Indian told them.

Sheriff Jackson picked up their guns and asked Indian to help him take the men to jail.

The next thing Indian knew was he was a deputy sheriff of St. Louis County, and when Sheriff Jackson asked his name he told him, "It's Johnny Able."

Indian knew he didn't want to be a lawman all his life, so he didn't want people to know his real name. He had seen what could happen to a lawman.

Indian kept practicing his fast draw, because now it seemed like he needed it almost every week. Being a quick draw meant he seldom ever had to fire his gun, since almost no one came close to getting their gun out of their holster before they were looking down the barrel of his gun aimed directly at them.

He stayed with that job for four years, but one day he told his friend Sheriff Jackson he was quitting because he wanted to go back home to Indian Territory and raise horses.

Sheriff Jackson asked him to stay several times before he left, but in the end the sheriff told him he should work at something he loved.

Indian thought about Sheriff Jackson a lot recently and wondered if he was still living or working. Indian liked him a lot, and he'd taught him several things about how to stay alive in a gunfight.

He was the one who told Indian that as fast a draw as he was, he should fall to the ground while he was pulling his gun. The sheriff said that it would always be a surprise to someone trying to shoot him, and on the ground, it made him a harder target to hit. It also gave him the advantage of using the ground to steady his weapon so he got a more accurate shot at a man standing in front of him.

Sheriff Jackson also told him, "When facing several men who are trying to shoot you, you first have to decide which one of the men is going to draw first. You will probably be able to know who's the fastest draw of the group by the way he acts or the way he carries his gun, and you can normally count on him to make his play first.

"After taking care of the first one, take the one next to him. After that, take your time to shoot straight at the ones left, 'cause they're going to be busy watching their friends fall and thinking they'll be next, and they will be if you take your time and shoot straight."

Sheriff Jackson was the one who told him about having a second gun he could draw sitting down; by using a special holster, he could draw the second gun cross-handed.

So Indian had the two matching hand-tooled leather holsters made when he worked in St. Louis, and they had worked well for him.

One thing on a trail drive you could be sure of was one or more of the drovers would have a guitar or a French harp to play every night around the campfire. Indian thought that was one of the best things about a trail drive.

He loved the music and the friendship you developed, regardless of how hard the work was. The men on a drive became your family.

In Texas you could be sure there was plenty of Mexican music, and there was something about the music that kept the cattle calm. Most of the drovers would sing softly as they watched over the herd at night. It helped to keep the herd quiet and kept the drover awake.

Few things surprised Indian anymore, but he was surprised by how well Serene was doing on this drive with her eastern upbringing.

She and Granny Hayes did everything that needed to be done by the trail drive cooks, and the men really liked Serene being with them on the trail.

Not only did he not have any problem with the men about her, but she was building a respect that you could never buy.

Not a lot of ranch owners nowadays made cattle drives with their herds, but here was Serene, the ranch owner, doing the cooking for them, and she was such a beautiful young woman and traveling right along with them. Indian thought that all of them would defend her with their lives.

The loyalty she was building was priceless. Indian was really proud of her.

Damn, he was thinking about her again—not that it was anything new. He spent a lot of time thinking about her. He was so taken with her, he could hardly think about anything else. He only wished he had some idea of what she thought about him.

He was determined to ask Serene how she felt about him and if she even liked him a little bit. He was going to try to have a romantic relationship with her. He didn't have much or any experience with romance, but for Serene, he was willing to try.

Adam Davis, his replacement night rider, came up behind him about that time and told him he was here to replace him. Indian thanked him and headed back to the campfire.

On arriving at the campsite, Indian was soon in his bedroll and sound asleep. He stayed that way until the sun was up and he began hearing the men getting up and talking about the day ahead of them.

One of the men, Carlos Espinal, said, "Good morning, Boss. Did you have a good sleep?"

Indian replied, "I don't know, Carlos. I think I was too busy sleeping."

Carlos only smiled at him and continued rolling up his bedroll so that it was ready to be stored in the chuck wagon for the day.

Indian realized another day had begun on The Great Western Trail.

Serene and Granny Hayes had coffee and breakfast ready before the men even started getting out of their bedrolls.

Indian could sure smell the coffee brewing and the biscuits baking in the Dutch oven.

By the time Indian got to the chuck wagon, Serene was already making her third huge pot of coffee. Many of the men had already finished their hearty breakfast, consuming a lot of strong black coffee, bacon, and several biscuits.

The men were just waiting for him to give them the word to start moving the cattle north toward Fort Griffin.

Indian said, "All of you better take a couple biscuits with you to help you make it through the day. It's going to be another long day in the saddle, and we've got another river to cross today."

He didn't have to say that more than once, as all the drovers picked up at least two biscuits and wrapped them in their kerchief and stuffed them in their pockets.

Crossing rivers meant a lot of extra work for everybody, and Indian's job today was to be sure he picked the right location for the crossing.

Picking the wrong place could cost the lives of steers and maybe upset the chuck wagon, making them lose their supplies or, worse yet, lose a man.

Adding to Indian's concern, at each river crossing of this trip he had to worry about something happening to Serene. She was his constant worry on this trip, and her driving a team and crossing rivers or creeks caused him even more worry than normal about her.

The other trick was to never let Serene know he was overly concerned about her, which was very hard for him to do.

As the drovers were leaving, Serene said, "Good morning, Indian. How are you this beautiful day?"

"Hungry!"

"That figures! So what can I get you?"

"My usual breakfast: biscuits, bacon, with lots of hot coffee." Serene replied, "You've got it, cowboy."

Serene handed him a plate filled with bacon and biscuits, and when she handed the plate to him, their hands touched.

Each of them quickly drew their hand back like they had just touched something really hot.

Serene blushed and said, "Indian, do you ever think about me?" "Only all the time, and after we get these cattle to market, I would like to see you. Do you know what I mean?"

"I think I know what you mean. Do you think you're falling in love with me?"

"Yes, but I don't know how you feel about me."

At that moment Granny Hayes came from the other side of the chuck wagon where she had been storing bedrolls in the wagon and getting things ready to leave. So Indian didn't get an answer to his question.

Granny said, "Indian, you better get your breakfast ate, because this chuck wagon is moving out."

Indian smiled and replied, "I think you're right, Granny. We got a long ways to go today."

Indian sat down, and in a few gulps he ate his breakfast like Granny told him. Then as he mounted his horse, he said, "I'll see you after I find a river crossing and be back to help you make the crossing."

CHAPTER EIGHT

TOO MANY RIVERS TO CROSS

SERENE WATCHED AS INDIAN rode away; she was thinking about her life and wondering if Indian was sent into her life because her father was killed by rustlers or that he might be the one man she could love and share her life with.

She knew there was something about him as when she was near him, she felt warm and excited. She had never had these feelings before. She didn't know if she should feel good about these feelings or be worried about them.

She only knew one thing; she liked the way she felt when he was near her!

Indian was riding hard to find a rocky crossing in the river for the chuck wagon to use. He certainly didn't want the chuck wagon getting stuck in the mud. That could cost them most of the day getting it out of the mud, and there was the danger of having it turn over in the river and losing all their supplies.

Indian rode for almost three hours before he reached the Colorado River and looked for a safe crossing for the herd and the chuck wagon. Indian knew all the rivers on The Great Western Trail, but he still had to check each one out before he committed the herd and chuck wagon to the crossing because at different times of the year, weather conditions could change where they crossed.

Indian thought back to the rivers they had already crossed on the trip: the Guadalupe River twice, the Pedernales, the Llano, and the San Saba. In Texas, they still had to cross the Clear Fork, Brazos, Wichita, Pease, and finally the Red River.

Then there were the rivers in Oklahoma Territory: Washita, Canadian, North Canadian, Cimarron, and Salt Fork River; and only the Arkansas in Kansas.

Anyway you looked at it, Indian thought there were too damn many rivers to cross. One problem with Texas rivers was that during different seasons of the year the crossings could never be in the same place. He had never attempted crossing the rivers this late in the year, so he couldn't just ride up to his normal crossing places.

When Indian arrived at the Colorado River, he began looking for a safe place for the chuck wagon to cross. It took him almost another hour before he found a place he felt good about to use for the crossing.

Indian started back to meet with Serene and Granny to guide them to the site he had chosen for them to take the chuck wagon across the river.

He had ridden for about an hour and half before he saw the chuck wagon.

Indian started waving at them, when suddenly he saw a band of about twelve Indians riding toward the chuck wagon. He urged his horse into a full run toward the chuck wagon.

When the Indians saw him coming, they slowed their pace and watched him keep riding at a full run toward the chuck wagon.

When Indian got closer, he saw Serene driving the team, but Granny was nowhere to be seen, and he wondered what had happened to her.

The Indians arrived at the chuck wagon at the same time that Indian did.

Indian greeted them in Comanche and then asked them if they were a hunting party.

Some of the Comanches recognized Leader and knew him to be a fair man and told him, "Yes." They had been hunting buffalo but didn't find any since the white man had killed too many buffalo.

The Comanches told him they wanted ten cows for crossing their land.

Indian told them they had a herd of cattle coming later in the day, and they would share a few cows with them.

Indian told them that he couldn't give them ten cows. He said he would give them three cows. They said, "No, we want ten cows." Indian said, "I can't give you more than five cows. That's fair payment for crossing your land."

They agreed. Indian told them to ride on to the river and wait until nightfall and he and the cows would be there. They agreed to do that, and they rode off in the direction of the river.

When they were out of sight, Indian asked Serene what happened to Granny.

Just then Granny appeared from the back of the wagon with her rifle in her hand saying, "Those redskins would have never known what hit them if they had tried anything with Serene."

The three of them laughed since there wasn't any major problem with the Comanches.

Indian told Serene, "The only problem for you is that I just gave away five of your cows."

She replied, "You can give them five more if it keeps them from causing us any trouble."

Indian said, "Well, they wanted ten cows, but I got them to take five. They will be waiting for them at the river when the herd gets there tonight."

Serene asked, "Don't you think they might try to take a lot more cattle having them waiting for the herd at the river tonight?" "No. I know a couple of these Comanches from dealing with them before. They will be happy with their five."

Indian said, "We need to get moving so I can help you get across the river to get started setting up camp for tonight."

When they arrived at the river, it took Indian a few minutes to locate the spot he planned to use for the chuck wagon to cross.

He guided his horse to the center of the crossing spot he chose and asked Serene to center her team of horses on his horse.

She followed his instructions and had a smooth crossing of the Colorado.

That was one less river he had to worry about Serene crossing, but they still had six more rivers to cross in Texas, five rivers in Indian Territory, and one in Kansas.

Serene and Granny were soon busy setting up camp for the night and starting dinner for their hungry crew.

Indian asked Granny to keep her Winchester close by in case the Indians came into camp since he had to be getting going to guide the herd to their location.

Before he left, he told Serene that he was glad they didn't have any big problems with the Comanches. As she walked him to his horse, he turned to her, pulled her close to him, and said, "Serene, I was so worried that something might happen to you. I'm really glad you're OK."

Then he leaned over and kissed her on her lips, got on his horse, and rode away at a trot. He had only gone a few feet away from her before he turned in his saddle and shouted, "I love you!"

Serene sat down on the grass and stared at him as he rode away, and said, "Wow, I never expected that!"

Granny said, "What did you say, child?" Serene just replied, "Wow!"

Granny said, "Yeah, that's what I thought you said."

It was over three hours before Indian and the herd made it back to the campsite. Serene and Indian looked at each other and neither knew quite what to say, so they just smiled at each other; both were lost in their own dreams.

Finally, Indian said to Serene and Granny, "We met your Comanches on the way here and gave them their five cows, and they went happily on their way."

Serene replied, "Good."

Nothing else was said between Indian and Serene that night.

CHAPTER NINE

ARRIVING AT FORT GRIFFIN

S O FAR, INDIAN WAS worried about crossing rivers with Serene driving the chuck wagon; it was one thing he needn't have worried about. After they crossed the Pedernales, they crossed the Colorado, Clear Fork, and the Brazos Rivers, and now they were within a few days of getting to Fort Griffin.

They had been on the trail now for sixty-five days, and Indian told Serene, "When we get to Fort Griffin, I want to give all of the men a chance to blow off a little steam."

He said, "They've got a little town just below the fort where they can get a drink and relax for a while before we begin to make the next leg of the trip. They been working hard and doing a good job, and they deserve some time off."

Serene asked him how he could let all the men have time off. He explained that he would let half of the men off a day at a time. "They will determine which day they got off by a drawing. Each man will draw a slip of paper that said either '1' or '2.'"

Three days later, Indian rode on to Fort Griffin to make sure there was room enough for the cattle to graze and not be too far away from the creek.

As he approached Fort Griffin, perched high up on a plateau, he thought to himself, "God, what a desolate-looking place," and he remembered what Robert E. Lee said when he was posted there as the deputy post commander: "It's not a fit place for man nor beast." Indian found a place for the cattle that still had some grass and was close enough to the creek. Indian rode past the fort to take a look at the little town located just north of the plateau.

It looked like there were still a few places operating; he stopped in front of the first saloon he came to and stepped down from his horse.

He slowly walked inside, and, as was his habit from his days as a deputy sheriff, he looked all around the room to see how many folks were in the saloon and where they were. Since the only person he saw in the saloon was the bartender, he made his way to the bar.

He slowly strolled up to the bar. The bartender asked him what he would like to drink.

Indian said, "Whiskey."

As the bartender delivered his drink, he asked, "Where you headed?"

"Dodge City."

The bartender remarked, "Dodge City! It's kind of late in the year to be going there, isn't it?"

"Yeah, it is, but I got a herd of cattle that will be coming by here in a day or two."

The bartender was surprised since they hadn't seen a trail herd for over a month come by Fort Griffin and said, "Boy, you're sure late pushing a herd to Dodge this time of the year, aren't you?

"I reckon we are, but my boss needs to get cattle to Dodge, so here we are."

"I'll be damned! Never thought I'd see another herd through here this late in the year. Well, I did have some fellers here a couple of weeks ago asking if I'd seen any herds coming through lately.

"Seems like they were looking for some trail boss by the name of Indian something-or-other. For some reason they really had to find him."

"What did these fellers look like?"

"Oh, I don't know. They looked like half the cowboys that come into this saloon. One thing for sure, they acted like he meant a lot to them for some reason."

"You don't know where they came from, do you?"

"No. They don't live around these parts. Even though I haven't been here too long, I know just about everyone that lives within a hundred miles or so from here."

"By the way, my name is Indian Leader. What's yours?"

"You're the feller those guys were looking for! Oh, my name is Paul Martin."

"Paul, I'm pretty sure I'm the one they were looking for, not too many people around named Indian."

"I guess you'd be right about that. I never heard of anyone named Indian before. How'd you come to get that name?"

"I was born in the Territory, so my folks named me Indian."
"I'll be damned!"

"We probably all are." Both men laughed at that.

Indian said thanks for the drink and told Paul, "My crew will probably be in to see you in a few days."

Indian was concerned that either Black Jack Eagle's men or some of the Phillips brothers were looking for him.

He didn't need either one of them right now; he had one big herd of cattle coming up the trail, and they were trouble enough.

Indian mounted his horse and set off at a gallop, wanting to get back to the herd and Serene as soon as he could.

A few miles south of Fort Griffin he heard a shot ring out and felt a hot pain in his right side; he rode only a short distance before he fell out of his saddle.

Indian hit the ground with a thud and rolled quite away from where he fell. He lay there in pain. He was trying to draw his gun from his left holster when he heard a horse approaching. He knew he had to get his gun out of his holster if he wanted to have any chance of staying alive.

Since he was lying on his gun, it was really hard to get his gun out of its holster.

Then he heard a horse stop next to him, and whoever had shot him was getting off his horse to finish him off.

The man kept his rifle pointed at Indian's back as he took his boot and put it under Indian and was slowly turning him over to be sure he was dead.

The man almost had Indian turned over to be sure he was dead.

Indian finished the last bit of his turning over himself and fired his gun directly at the man standing over him.

Indian shot the man directly under his chin, and the bullet went through his brain and out through the top of his head, driving the man backward and down on his back before he had a chance to fire his gun again.

Indian saw the bullet exiting out of the top his head; he was dead before he hit the ground.

Indian couldn't believe who had shot him because even with the condition of his shot-up face, Indian could see it was the bartender, Paul—but why?

Slowly, Indian managed to get to his feet. He began looking for his horse, which was standing a short distance away. Indian called for his horse to come to him, and the horse did.

Slowly, Indian tried to pull himself up on his horse, but the pain was too much and Indian fell back on the ground. Indian lay there for what he thought was a long time.

When he opened his eyes, he saw it was already dark.

He was relieved to see his horse still standing next to him, waiting for him.

Although it was very hard for Indian to speak, he said to his horse, "Good boy."

Indian took the reins in his left hand, got his left foot up in the stirrup, and took a firm hold of the saddle horn. He tried again to pull himself up on the saddle. This time he managed to swing his right leg over his saddle and made it up on his saddle.

He turned his horse south, back toward a bright star he saw in the sky, about where he thought the herd and Serene should be.

It was already dark, and there were two things he didn't know: one, could he find Serene, and two, he didn't know how long he could stay in the saddle.

The one thing he knew for sure was he was hurting pretty bad, and riding wasn't helping his pain. He put his neckerchief against his wound and held it as tight as he could.

As Indian rode, he kept going in and out of consciousness, but his horse continued going in the same direction as Indian headed him; he knew that because he could still see the bright star in front of him—it was leading him back to Serene.

He had no idea how long he had been riding, but it seemed liked he had been riding for a really long time. He kept slumping farther down on his saddle; by now, his head was leaning against his horse's neck.

The next thing he knew was his horse stopped, and he fell off. He heard voices yelling his name, and he passed out.

Granny Hayes yelled to Serene, "Indian's been shot!"

Serene ran to where Indian lay and got down on her knees beside him; she asked Granny, "Is he dead?"

Granny felt his chest and replied, "No, but we need to get him over by the fire so I can see how bad his wound is. I can see and feel blood all on the side of his shirt."

Serene told two cowboys, "Carry Indian by the fire so Granny can take a look at his wound!"

The cowboys picked Indian up and carefully carried him to the campfire.

Granny knelt down next to him and pulled his shirt out of his pants so she could see where the wound was in his side.

Granny said, "Well, the bullet came in and went out. That's good news. I don't think it hit any organs. It's just a flesh wound, but he's lost a lot of blood from the looks of his shirt and pants.

"We need to get him up into the wagon so I can dress the wound. I think he's stopped bleeding. That's good news."

Serene told the cowboys to get him up in the wagon.

She climbed up in the wagon and lit a lantern, and four cowboys lifted Indian up inside the wagon.

Serene had laid blankets out to make a bed for Indian, and the cowboys laid him down on it.

By this time, Granny was in the wagon with her medical kit, and she began cleaning up his wound as Serene watched.

"Granny, do you think he's going to be all right?"

"Child, don't you worry. He's tough as nails. He'll be OK. It might take a few days, but you can be sure he will be back in the saddle very soon."

"I sure hope so. We need him."

"Yeah, we need him, and you need him too, don't you, child?"

"Sure I need him. He's the only one who knows how to get the cattle to Dodge City."

"I don't think that's all you need him for."

Serene blushed and replied, "Granny, you're a troublemaker."

"I see how you two look at each other all the time. You know, I wasn't born yesterday. I know those looks. Right now we got to get these boots and pants off so we can get them and his shirt washed up."

Serene began pulling off his boots as Granny unfastened his gun belt and the belt on his pants.

Granny said, "Pull down his britches, girl, while I lift him up." Serene began slowly pulling down his pants.

Granny said, "Girl, hurry up he's heavy. You act like you never pulled down a man's pants before. Come to think about it, you probably never have."

Serene didn't answer. She finished taking Indian's pants off, picked up his shirt, and tried to decide how she could wash them tonight.

Granny said, "We'll have to wait till morning to wash them. You'll need to go through his saddlebags to see if you can find him another shirt and a pair of pants for him."

Serene got out of the wagon and asked the cowboys what they had done with Indian's saddle and saddlebags.

They showed her where his things were lying at the rear of the chuck wagon.

They asked how bad Indian was hurt.

Serene replied, "Granny says he was lucky 'cause the bullet just went through his side and didn't hit any vital organs, but he lost a lot of blood and it's going to take him a few days to get back on his feet."

The cowboys sighed with relief; they were concerned because without him they didn't think they would be able to make it to Dodge.

Indian was the trail boss because he knew the way and what it took to get them and the herd there.

Truth be known, they were more worried about them making it safely there and back home again than if the cattle got to Dodge.

Serene searched through his saddlebags and found another pair of pants and a shirt. She thought she would never put on clothes that were this wrinkled.

She wondered if she might be lucky enough on this trip to have a clean outfit to put on by the time they got to Dodge.

She looked down at her dress, and even in the dark she could see it was covered with dust and dirt. There was no way to stay clean or get clean on a cattle drive.

Granny cleaned and dressed Indian's wound, and she sewed up the skin where the bullet had entered and exited his body.

Granny was certainly thankful Indian was unconscious when she sewed up his wounds, for both of their sakes.

Serene climbed back up into the wagon and helped Granny put Indian's shirt and pants on, but they left his boots off.

Granny said, "I'm going take my bedroll and sleep next to the fire, and you stay here and watch over Indian for the night."

Granny picked up her bedroll, threw it on the ground, climbed out of the wagon, and fixed her a bed next to the fire.

Serene lay down next to Indian and wondered if this would be the only time she would ever be lying next to him. Then she made herself quit thinking and soon fell asleep.

CHAPTER TEN

GOOD MORNING, INDIAN

MORNING CAME QUICKLY LIKE it did every morning on the cattle drive. Serene opened her eyes and looked over at Indian sleeping next to her and saw his arm was around her butt.

When she moved his arm, Indian opened his eyes and saw Serene lying next to him. He didn't say anything; he just stared at her. He didn't know where he was and why he was there next to Serene.

Serene casually said, "Good morning, Indian. How do you feel this morning?"

Indian took his hand and softly touched her face and said, "I thought I must have died and I was in heaven with you lying beside me, but you're real."

"Yeah, I'm real all right, and you're not in heaven. You still leading a cattle drive to Dodge, cowboy?"

Indian sat up and felt the pain in his side. Yeah, he remembered everything now except how he got in the wagon and had Serene lying beside him.

"Granny and I got you cleaned up and changed your clothes. Granny said you should be OK in a couple of days."

Indian looked at his clothes and saw he had on different clothes than he had on yesterday and said, "You mean you changed my clothes? Where's my boots?"

"Well, yes, I helped Granny change your clothes, and your boots are right here." She picked them up and showed them to him.

Indian felt embarrassed and didn't know what to say. Finally he said, "Thank you. Now I better get my boots on and get back to work moving your cattle."

"Not so fast, cowboy. Are you sure you're ready to go back to work?"

"I don't know, but I can't lie around here with you all day either. Although I would have to say I would really like to."

Indian felt embarrassed again and couldn't believe he had blurted that out. Although he meant exactly what he said, he knew he had no right saying it.

He stammered, "I'm sorry, Serene."

She shot back, "What are you sorry for? Sorry you said it, or that you'd be sorry you had to lie here with me all day?"

Indian was perplexed; he didn't know what to say, so he said nothing. Serene was just too fast a wit for him to keep up with. He was just a simple cowboy.

He asked if Serene would help him with his boots because he didn't think he could lean down far enough to get his boots on.

She helped him to put on his boots and said, "I've got to get to work myself helping Granny fix breakfast.

"Indian, are you sure you're able to get out of the wagon and ride a horse today?"

"I'm damn sure going to try." "How did you get shot anyway?"

"I know how I got shot, but I sure don't know why I got shot." "What are you saying?"

"After I found where we would keep the cattle at Fort Griffin, I stopped at a saloon in the little town below the fort and had a drink. The bartender told me some guys had been in a few weeks ago asking if I had been in there. They said they really needed to find me.

"I left the saloon and was riding back to meet you, and somebody shot me with a rifle from some distance away. The bullet hit me in my right side. After I was shot, my horse went a little ways, and I fell off my horse, and when the person who shot me came to check to make sure I was dead, I shot and killed him. It was the bartender.

"I have no idea why he would want to kill me. I never saw him before in my life. Damned if I know why he would shoot me.

"After some time went by, I was able to get back on my horse and started riding back to meet you and the herd."

Serene said, "I know why he shot you. It's spelled M-O-N-E-Y! I would say somebody doesn't want you to keep living, or they don't want you to get my cattle to Dodge so I can pay my loan off, one or the other.

"Whichever it is, it's not good. You're going to have to be careful telling people who you are on this drive, because if they offered the bartender money to kill you, they're bound to keep making offers to more people along the route."

"Serene, I guess you're right. We just don't know which one it is."

Indian was determined to get out of the chuck wagon and get on his horse and not to let a little bullet wound in his side slow him down. Foolish man that he was, he tried to stand up and fell right back from where he had just got up.

Serene asked "Can I help you get up?"

"I guess you will have to. I don't seem to be able to do it by myself."

Serene took hold of his right hand as Indian tried a second time to get up; this time he made it up and fell right into Serene's arms.

She said, "Are you sure you're able to do this? You're pretty weak, cowboy!"

"I'm sure I can. We've got a long way to go, and if I can't ride, I'm not going to be much use to you."

Serene turned her face up to look directly at Indian's; she could see the pain in his eyes.

She started to tell him he had no business getting out of bed, but then he leaned down and kissed her lips.

At first she tried to move away from Indian, but since she was holding him up she couldn't move away without him falling.

Suddenly, she didn't know why, but she started kissing him back, and just as suddenly as she did, he pulled away from her and said, "Serene, I'm sorry. I shouldn't have done that."

Serene replied, Oh, I think you should have!"

Then she leaned up to kiss him, and when she did, he met her lips like a hungry lion ready to devour his prey. This time neither of them was sorry.

They continued kissing and holding on to each other until Granny pulled back the canvas flap on the wagon and asked, "How's Indian?"

When she saw them kissing, she said, "A helluva lot better, I see!"

Granny closed the flap and went back to fixing breakfast. Serene and Indian broke away from each other and then just stood for a little while looking into each other's eyes. They just kept smiling at each other like they were pleased about something they had accomplished.

Finally, Serene said, "I guess I better help Granny fix breakfast."

Indian continued smiling at her and replied, "I guess you better."

"Yeah, I better."

Serene climbed out of wagon and started working like she had been doing every day since they began the cattle drive.

Neither Serene nor Granny said a thing about the kiss Granny saw.

Several minutes later, Indian cautiously got down from the wagon and spoke to Granny and thanked her for taking care of his wound.

Granny said, "I'm glad the wound wasn't any worse than it was and am glad you're doing better."

Then she smiled at him and asked if he was ready for breakfast. He certainly was and ate everything she put in front of him and downed several cups of hot black coffee.

Indian asked Teddy to saddle him a horse.

After Teddy returned with his horse, Indian climbed up in the saddle and rode off to pick out a campsite for that night.

As he rode along, he kept thinking about the kisses he and Serene had shared and how he felt warm and wanted more of her kisses. He loved how he felt on holding and kissing her. Not only did he want more of her kisses, but he wanted more, much more; he wanted her.

After riding for about ten miles, he saw buzzards circling high in the sky ahead of him. He wasn't sure how much farther they were from his current position, but he guessed they were still several miles ahead of him.

He thought they must be circling above the body of the bartender who had tried to kill him yesterday.

Indian was sorry he wasn't up to burying him yesterday, but then he wasn't in any condition to do it. He thought he would take care of that tomorrow. He would have his drovers do it if the damn buzzards left enough of his body to bury.

Indian rode on a little bit further and found a good location for their campsite and turned his horse around to go back to Serene and the herd.

As he turned his horse around, he could still see the buzzards circling high in the sky in front of him.

As he rode back to the herd, he kept thinking that it could have been him lying there with the buzzards circling over his body if that bartender had been just a little bit better shot.

He thought about his life and remembered his kisses with Serene that morning. He now realized how much he had missed in his life—to love someone and have someone who loved him.

He quickly came to the conclusion he wasn't going to keep missing out on the love of a good woman.

He hoped Serene felt the same as he did. He realized something else—he had fallen in love with her the moment they met for the first time; he just didn't know it then.

He put his horse into a gallop. He wanted to get back to Serene as soon as he could. He had to tell her he loved her.

CHAPTER ELEVEN

THE CATTLE DRIVE'S BIG CHANGE

WHEN INDIAN SAW THE chuck wagon coming, he put his horse into a full run so he could get to Serene as quickly as he could.

Serene and Granny saw Indian riding as fast as his horse could carry him and knew there must be something really wrong.

When Indian got close to the wagon, Serene yelled, "What's wrong?"

Indian pulled his horse to a stop next to the wagon and said, "Nothing, except I have to talk to you right now!"

Serene got down from the wagon, and as Indian took his foot out of the stirrup, he told her to get on the horse with him. She put her foot up in the stirrup; he reached for her hand and pulled her up on the horse behind him, and they rode off.

Granny watched all of this and just stared at them without saying a word. She wondered what was happening.

After riding a little way from the wagon, Indian stopped his horse and asked Serene to get off. He got off his horse, grabbed her with both arms, pulled her as close to him as he could get her, and kissed her harder than she had ever been kissed in her life.

After a few minutes he released her and said, "Serene, I love you and want to be with you the rest of my life."

"Whoa, cowboy! Do you know what you're saying?" "I do. I want you to be my wife!"

"OK, but give me a minute or two to think about it, OK?" "OK, but I had to tell you now how I feel about you before I couldn't get the words out." "Well, you told me."

"Serene, do you love me? Do you want to marry me?" "I do, and I will!"

"Good! That's settled. We'll get married as soon as we get to Dodge."

"How long will it be before we get to Dodge?" "The way I feel right now, too damned long!" Serene laughed.

Indian said, "I love the way you laugh. It's musical." "You say that just because you love me."

"Well, I sure do love you!"

"Indian, don't you think we better get the chuck wagon moving so we can get camp set up?

"Granny and I have to start fixing supper for the crew." "Yes, I do."

Indian got back on his horse and helped Serene get up behind him. They rode back to where they had left Granny and the chuck wagon.

Serene got off the horse and climbed back on the wagon where Granny was waiting.

Indian started riding north toward the campsite he had chosen for the night.

Granny asked, "What in the world was that all about, child?" "Nothing much. Indian just asked me to marry him."

"Oh, is that all?" "That's all."

"OK, so what did you say?"

"Nothing much. I just told him I would."

"You told him you'd marry him! Are you sure you know what you're doing?"

"No. I'm not sure I know what I'm doing, except I know I love him."

"I reckon that's a helluva good reason to marry him, even if he happens to be tall and good-looking and has a wonderful smile. I guess loving him is a good enough reason to marry him."

Serene didn't say anything else; she just kept driving the team, following where Indian was leading them.

As Indian rode along, every few minutes he kept looking back at Serene; he sure liked what he saw. Serene was wonderful to look at, and he couldn't wait to marry her.

He kept thinking about how lucky he was to find her; she was smart, educated back east, and pretty too.

He thought, "Well, maybe she isn't too smart after all. She did agree to marry me, didn't she? And I'm just a cowboy who can hardly read and write."

He was sure she had a lot of men back east that would be more suited for her and certainly be more in her class. Serene had real class!

He was certainly happy she loved him like he loved her; he just hoped that would be enough to keep her happy.

An hour later, they arrived at the campsite Indian had picked out for their stop for the night.

Indian could still see the buzzards circling north of them where the body of the dead bartender lay.

Indian didn't say anything about the buzzards to the two women.

He said, "This is home for the night, ladies. While you're getting the camp set up and fixing supper, I'll be riding back to the herd to guide them here."

Indian turned his horse south and rode off at a gallop.

Serene and Granny began setting up camp and fixing the evening meal. It was the same drill every night: get the men's bedrolls out of the wagon and start a fire, which sometimes wasn't too easy because wood wasn't easy to find along the trail. When they did find some, they loaded as much as they could into the wagon.

They were getting low on several items they needed for fixing meals, like coffee and beans. No trail drive could do without these essentials. The drovers' staples were beef, beans, biscuits, and coffee.

They certainly had plenty of cattle to choose from for the beef, but they needed more beans and coffee.

Serene couldn't even guess how many gallons of coffee they had made since the drive started. She needed to tell Indian they needed to go shopping whenever they could find some place to get coffee and beans.

Over an hour and half went by before Serene saw Indian and the point men bringing up the front of the herd.

She watched as Indian began turning the lead Longhorns, and she thought he sat in the saddle like he were part of the horse.

God, it was beautiful the way he turned the cattle to get the herd stopped and bedded down for the night. She thought he was like an artist painting a masterpiece; no extra moves were made by him or his horse, and the cattle responded just like paint on a master artist's paintbrush.

The lead cattle stopped, turned, and began grazing, and when the next bunch of cattle arrived, they did exactly what the leaders did. They stopped, turned, and began grazing.

Each new group of cattle behaved the same way when they arrived at the herd. It took several hours before the last of the herd of over three thousand Longhorns arrived, and the riders riding drag were finally able to get their supper.

When most of the drovers were having supper, Serene said, "I have some good news to tell everyone."

The drovers, who had been talking about their day, quit talking so they could hear what the boss lady had to say.

"I just wanted to tell everyone that when we get to Dodge, you're all invited to a wedding because Indian and I are going to get married."

There was dead silence for a moment; it even seemed like the cows stopped making noise.

Then Granny said, "That's wonderful, Serene. Don't you all think so, boys?"

The drovers all started clapping and yelling, "Wonderful, yeah, that's wonderful!"

Indian had been standing near the chuck wagon just listening when suddenly all the men were shaking his hand, pounding him on his back, and saying, "Way to go, Boss! Way to go!"

Before going to bed that night, Indian told Serene that when they got to their stopping place at Fort Griffin, he was giving all the drovers a couple of days off. He said, "We will give half of the crew off one day, and the other half of the crew the following day."

He said he would have the men draw a slip of paper out of his hat—with a number on it, either a one or a two—to determine which day they got off to go to town.

CHAPTER TWELVE

DAYS OFF ON A CATTLE DRIVE

T HE NEXT DAY INDIAN took two of his drovers and a couple of shovels to help bury the bartender he had killed when he went to check for a location for a campsite near Fort Griffin.

He didn't really want Serene and Granny to see what the buzzards may have left of his body.

The drovers were shocked at what they saw; it wasn't a pretty sight. One of the men lost his breakfast after seeing what buzzards could do to a human body when it was left out in the open for a couple of days.

Indian helped as much as he could, which wasn't a lot since he still healing from the shot in his side from two days ago. He was healing better than he should this soon, thanks to Granny's doctoring.

After they finished burying the bartender, they returned to the herd and resumed their normal duties.

Indian told Serene and Granny that today they would have a shorter trip than normal, since they had traveled further than he planned to yesterday.

He said, "Today we should get into camp early enough for you to go to town and buy the supplies you need."

Both of them felt really good about not traveling as far as they normally did every day and felt even better about being able to restock their supplies.

Arriving at the location of their new campsite, the two women started unloading the drovers' bedrolls and much of the cooking equipment from the wagon to give them room for their new supplies. The work of unloading the wagon went faster than normal with Indian helping them.

Granny said, "Careful, Trail Boss, we'll be expecting your help to unload the wagon at every campsite from now on."

Indian smiled and replied, "Don't get your hopes up too high. This is a one-time deal!"

"Yeah, just what I'd expect!" Granny shot back at Indian.

Then she said, "Girl, you can see what kind of help you can expect to get after you're married. Just like every husband in the world, they expect you to have the kids and do all the work."

Serene asked, "Is that how it was with your husband, Granny?" "Hell, no! I had a jewel for a husband. He looked after me all the time. He helped me with my work. He even helped me look after the kids, but he was one in a million."

"Well, Granny, maybe my Indian will be one in a million too." "I sure hope so, girl."

Indian kept his mouth shut during this conversation, but finally he said, "OK, ladies, if you are through beating up on all the husbands of the world, I'll go with you to show you the way to town and help you get your supplies."

Granny and Serene got in the wagon at the same time Indian climbed back on his horse. Then he turned his horse toward the town, and Serene followed him.

It took them about thirty minutes to get to town.

Indian stopped his horse in front of the general store, and Serene parked the wagon right behind his horse.

Serene tied the lines of her horses to the brake lever on the wagon. Then Granny and she went directly into the store with Indian following right behind them.

Once Serene was in the store, she began ordering the supplies they needed as Granny keep track of each item she ordered to be sure Serene didn't miss anything.

While Serene was busy placing her order, Indian looked around the store and decided he needed some more bullets for his six-guns. He also decided he could use another shirt since his had a bullet hole through the side.

He was glad it wasn't his buckskin shirt he was wearing when he got shot; he loved the buckskin outfits his mother made for him.

He knew she wasn't his real mother, but she was the only mother he remembered and he loved her and his dad. He was so damn lucky to have them for his folks; they took him in and raised him. He knew they loved him too.

He was going to have to take Serene to meet them very soon because they were getting up in years, and you never knew how much longer they might live.

Soon the store clerk had all of Serene's order ready and helped her out to the wagon with their supplies, and then he came back in the store to wait on Indian.

Indian asked for two boxes of shells and paid for them and his shirt. Then he went outside where Serene and Granny were waiting.

As Serene was getting ready to get back up on the wagon, a couple of army officers walked past them. One of them stopped and came back and said, "Serene Star, is that you?"

Serene looked at the young man and replied, "Yes, I'm Serene Star. Who are you?" "Jack Whitman."

"Jack! What in the world are you doing out here?"

He replied, "Well, it's Captain Jack Whitman now. I'm posted at Fort Griffin. So what are you doing here?"

"I'm on a cattle drive taking a herd of my Longhorns to Dodge."

"I can't believe you're on a cattle drive, a lady like you. I've seen a lot of cattle moved through this area, but none of them had a beautiful woman like you with them. From what I have observed, that's about as tough a life as one might encounter."

"I can tell you it's not like going on a picnic in Central Park in New York City, but my father was killed by rustlers, and I have to sell some cattle to pay off a debt."

"Serene, can you have dinner with me at the fort tonight? It's not like dining in one of our restaurants in New York either, but it's the best we can do here."

"Jack, I'd like to introduce you to the man I'm about to marry. Jack, this is Indian Leader, Indian, this is my friend from college, Jack Whitman."

Indian reached out his hand to Jack, and Jack shook his hand with a very firm grip.

Jack then said, "My dinner offer is certainly extended to you. I do hope you can both join me for dinner tonight."

Serene replied, "Jack, I'm sure it would be nice, but I'm afraid it's not possible. I have too much to do helping to get supper ready for our drovers.

"Maybe you could come out to our campsite. It's down by the creek, and you can have supper with us. I'm sure it won't be as elegant as you might be able to provide to us at the fort, but we would enjoy visiting with you about how you got into the army and posted in this place."

"What time would you like me to be there?" "Six thirty would be good."

"Great! I'll see both of you at six thirty."

With that Captain Jack Whitman gave Serene a salute and turned to join his companion, who had been waiting for him with their horses.

*****

Indian managed to concoct a dinner table out of the stump of a tree and rolled up some rather large logs for benches on each side of the stump.

Serene found a piece of white material which had been brought along to be used as bandages to use as a tablecloth.

Granny and Serene polished the metal plates and silverware the best they could for Serene's dinner guest and used part of the white bandage material for napkins.

Granny said, "What could your friend Jack expect with you on a trail drive for goodness' sake, girl? I would say your makeshift table looks pretty damn good with what you got to work with."

"Yes, I know, Granny, but Jack's family are some of richest people in the country. You should have seen their home and the beautiful silver and china they used for the meals they served when I was a guest in their home. It was like being in china and silver shops every meal."

"OK, Serene, it was wonderful, but what the heck is a rich boy like that doing in the army in this part of the country? If he was going to be in the army, why isn't he in some place like Washington?"

"I don't know, Granny. I doubt he had ever been west of New York City before in his life."

A few minutes before six thirty Jack arrived at their campsite as Serene and Granny were finishing fixing dinner.

Jack and the first group of drovers arrived at the campsite almost at the same time.

Granny told Serene she would look after the drovers, and she should take care of Jack, Indian, and herself.

Indian greeted Jack and took care of his horse as Serene finished filling their plates and showing Jack where to sit.

She sat down next to Indian and began asking Jack questions about people they knew.

Indian felt like he was a stranger overhearing a conversation between two people who knew each other well while he was sitting at another table.

He understood that it was good for Serene to hear about her old friends, but it made him feel very uncomfortable. He sat there wondering if hearing and thinking about the wonderful places and friends she had back east would make her lose interest in him.

Life sounded so much easier and more fun-filled back there than herding a bunch of dumb Longhorns from Texas to Dodge.

Finally, Serene asked Jack the question that she really wanted answered, "Jack, what made you join the army and be stationed out west?"

The expression on Jack's faced turned instantly from laughing and smiling to dead sober, and he took some time before he attempted an answer.

Jack answered tearfully, "After we finished school, I went into business with my father. You know he's in a lot of different businesses. I chose to work in our bank in New York and loved getting to meet so many types of people and be able to help them when they need money.

"I don't know if you remember Betty Townsend, since she was in the class behind ours, but we fell in love and got married. On what would have been our first anniversary, she was having our baby. Both she and our baby died. She died in childbirth, and the baby was stillborn.

"I had to get away as far as I could from everyone and everything I knew, so I joined the army and volunteered to come to Texas.

"Well, I certainly got away, ending up in this place!" "Jack, I'm so sorry to hear about your wife and child." Jack was doing his best trying not to cry.

Indian felt really sorry about him losing his wife and baby. It was awful.

The three of them continued to sit there for several minutes without saying a word before Jack said, "Serene, I was happy to see you again and want to thank you for a wonderful dinner. It's getting late, and I need to get back to the fort."

Jack got up from the log, and Indian went to get his horse for him.

When Indian returned with his horse, Serene was holding Jack and telling him that she was so sorry about his wife and baby.

When Jack saw Indian had brought him his horse, he broke away from Serene and thanked her again for dinner and thanked Indian for sharing the evening with him.

Indian said, "Jack, I'm sorry you lost your loved ones, and I hope we meet again someday."

After Jack was on his horse he said to Indian, "You've got a wonderful woman who's going to be your wife. I would have married her in a minute if she would have had me, but she was only interested in coming back to her ranch in Texas."

Then Jack said, "Serene, thank you for listening to my story about Betty and my baby. It's the first time I could tell anybody about it. It has really helped me to say it out loud. Now maybe the pain will be easier for me. I love you, you know."

"I know, Jack. I love you, too."

Jack turned his horse back toward the fort and rode off into the night.

Serene reached out her arms to Indian, and he took her in his arms and held her as close as he could and she said, "I do love Jack. He is a very special person to me, but there are many types of love. I love you the way a woman loves a man she needs and wants for her husband, and, cowboy, that's you!"

They kissed and held each other for long time, hoping neither of them died without having many, many years together.

*****

The next morning, the men who drew a "one" saddled up and rode into town to enjoy their day off from the trail drive. The men who drew a "two" spent their day thinking about how they would spend their day off tomorrow and hoping the first bunch of men didn't drink all the whiskey and catch all the women.

Granny was working on catching up on some mending for several of the cowboys, and Serene and Indian rode off to the east to have some time away from everyone.

The day was warm and sunny for this time of the year, so it was a good day to be alive.

Serene and Indian intended to spend the day enjoying each other in each other's arms and just enjoy being alive.

CHAPTER THIRTEEN

ON THE TRAIL AGAIN

TWO DAYS LATER AND without any problems with any of his men in town, Indian and the cattle drive was on the move again. All the men and livestock seemed to be moving with a little quicker step this morning.

The horses and cattle got a chance to feed on whatever grass they could find around the creek, and both men and animals had a chance for a bit of rest. The men didn't eat dirt and dust all day as they had for so many days on the drive.

Indian was pleased that no one had problems in town, and he thought the mood of the men was much better after having a day off.

He had been pushing everyone pretty hard on this drive, including Serene and Granny.

They were both real troopers to get up before everyone else, travel by themselves for most of the day, and then have camp set up and the evening meal ready for the men when the day's drive was over.

They were doing a great job!

Indian left the campsite before the last of the men finished their breakfast to check on the best place for today's river crossing and find somewhere to set up camp for the night.

From now until they got to Dodge, the chance of getting rain or snow became more likely every day.

Indian could feel the weather changing; it was getting a little colder every night, and they still had a long way to go.

Indian was doing well on his ride today and was covering the miles at a very steady pace, all the time thinking about Serene's friend, Jack. He really felt sorry for him.

Losing his wife and baby on the day of their first wedding anniversary—unbelievable!

Life sure didn't seem fair; no matter how much money you had or didn't have, so many awful things could happen to you or your loved ones.

Indian's horse picked up a stone or something in his right front hoof and started limping.

Indian stopped him and got off to check out the problem, but as he was dismounting, he heard a bullet pass over his head.

A second shot hit his horse right in the head, and his horse fell dead.

Bullets were hitting the ground all around him as Indian lay as close to his dead horse as he could get.

Indian finally spotted where the bullets were coming from. He saw two men up on a small ridge about hundred and fifty yards away from him.

Then he saw the two men get on their horses and begin riding as fast as their horses could carry them directly at him.

Indian had his two six-guns out ready and waiting for them, but he wasn't going to be in any hurry to shoot at them. He would wait until they drew nearer.

As they were coming fast, it wouldn't take them long to be in range of his six-guns.

Indian didn't know who these two men were, but they would have shot him if his horse hadn't picked up something in his hoof.

Indian continued to lie very still behind his dead horse waiting for them, but they did something he didn't expect: they separated, one going to his right and the other one going to his left.

No matter, he could still get them. He was lying in a prone position, and they were on moving horses. His chances of getting the more accurate shots were a lot better than what they would have riding on their horses.

Just as they passed his dead horse, he fired the pistol in his right hand at the man on his right; then he fired the pistol in his left hand at the man on his left.

Neither of them had a chance to fire a shot at him; they were both slumped backward on their horses from the impact of his bullets hitting them.

A short time later, both the men fell off their horses.

The horses ran a few more feet and stopped, waiting for their riders to direct them.

Indian was certainly happy they stopped, because it would have been a long walk back to find his people.

Indian continued lying where he was to be sure there weren't any more men coming after him.

When he didn't see anyone else coming, he got up and walked over to where the first gunman lay on his right. The man was lying on his back, and Indian could see he had hit him near his heart; there was no question about it. This man was dead.

Next, Indian walked over to where the second man lay, and Indian could see that this man was dead too. He had shot him in the head just a little left of being dead center between his eyes.

Indian didn't have any idea who these men were.

He caught up with one of the horses, mounted him, and rode over and picked up the other horse.

Indian looked over their brand and saw it was the same brand as the horses he let loose after killing the two brothers from Cedar City, the ones that had come after him for killing their brother Billy.

If these were two more of the brothers, there were only three brothers left out of the seven brothers he was told Billy had.

If they kept coming after him and he kept killing them, soon there wouldn't be any of the brothers left.

If he didn't have to get Serene's cattle to market, he thought he might as well go back to Cedar City and have it out with the other three brothers and get it over with.

Right now he couldn't think about doing such a thing. He had a chuck wagon with Serene and Granny in it and three thousand head of Longhorns following him. He had lost time needed to find a safe river crossing and a place for his outfit to bed down for the night.

No chance of going back to Cedar City now; he had his hands full.

Also, he had to do something to be sure he stayed alive. There were lots of people depending on him. Besides, he was going to get married when he got to Dodge.

He had way too much to live for to get himself killed. It wasn't his fault he had killed these men's brother. After all, he just defended himself when their brother Billy tried to kill him.

He didn't have any way to bury these two, but he took the time to pick up their guns and gun belts; he checked their pockets for identification, money or any other valuables they might have, and when he had time, he would send it back to their families.

He was shocked to find that between them, they had almost five hundred dollars and each had a gold watch; these two men sure weren't just a couple of cowboys sent to kill him.

He also found a couple of telegrams in their pockets from the bartender telling them that the man they were looking for was in town.

Yeah, they were certainly two more of Billy's brothers. Damn, he could sure use somebody to help him stay alive.

He had to get Serene's cattle to Dodge so she didn't lose her ranch, and they could get married.

Before he got back on one of the horses, he took his saddle and saddlebags off his dead horse and changed them for the ones on the horse he intended to ride.

He put the guns and the other things he took from the two dead men in the saddlebags on the extra horse and tied on the two rifles, one on each side of the saddle.

The last thing he had to do was to tie a lead rope on the halter of the extra horse to the saddle horn of his saddle.

Morning was already gone, and he hadn't accomplished one thing he had set out to do today.

Well, he guessed he had accomplished the most important thing to do for the day; he stayed alive!

Indian took one more look around before starting out to find his river crossing and their campsite for the night.

Seeing no one else around to cause him harm, Indian galloped out to do the work he had set out to do.

He soon found a location on the river with a nice rocky bottom; it was perfect for the wagon to cross, and not too far from there, he found a good place for tonight's campsite.

It looked like it had been used by several cattle drives this year. The grass was worn down around the area, and he could see some old wagon tracks. There was even some wood left for a fire.

Finding what he needed, he started back to find the herd and Serene to guide them to this location.

It took Indian almost three hours of hard riding before he could see the chuck wagon and the leading group of Longhorns not far behind the wagon.

When Indian got up to the chuck wagon Serene asked, "Where did you get the extra horse?"

"I had some trouble this morning; a couple of men tried to kill me. They killed my horse, so I had to take their horses to get back to you."

"What happened to the men?"

"I had to kill them. They didn't want me to take their horses."

"Indian, are you sure you are all right?"

"I'm fine. I'm just a little late getting back to you, but I did find a place to cross the river and a campsite for tonight.

"Serene, it looks like you are a little late in getting started this morning since I can see the herd not very far behind you, what happened?"

"Well, we had a little wheel problem from crossing so many rivers, I guess. The hubs were so dry that we had to pull off the front wheels and grease the hubs. That slowed us down a lot."

"You mean you and Granny took the wheels off by yourself?"

"No, we had to get some of the men to help us raise up the wagon, one wheel at a time, using the stump and the logs you used for our table and benches last night.

"We were able to use the tree stump for leverage and some big tree limbs to raise the front of the wagon up one side at a time. Then we used the logs we used for our benches last night to put under the axle to hold the wagon up so we could take the wheel off."

"I'm really glad you were able to get the problem fixed and get back on the trail as quick as you did."

"I think we did good getting the problem fixed before we broke down."

"How about the rear wheels? Are they OK?"

"We checked them, and you could still see grease coming out around the hub. So we think they are OK."

"Good."

"We need to get a move on to get you across the river and to the campsite before it gets much darker.

"Granny, whip your team up and let's get going."

"OK, Boss man. Here we go!" Granny said. She snapped her whip over the head of her team, and they began to run.

Indian urged his horses on to keep up with the wagon and then to get in front of it to guide them to the spot he had chosen for their river crossing.

After several minutes of an all-out dead run by his horses and the chuck wagon team, Indian began slowing down his horses, and Granny reined in her team back to a brisk walk. They continued at this pace until they arrived at the location he had chosen to take the wagon across the river.

As was his normal way of helping them to cross rivers, Indian guided his horses into the river crossing to lead them across the river, using the rocky bottom of the river.

Granny pulled the team in a path directly behind Indian and followed his horses across the river without any problem or delay.

Reaching the other side of the river, Indian led them on to the campsite he had chosen.

Arriving at the campsite, Indian dismounted his horse and as soon as the wagon came to a stop, Serene was off the wagon and into Indian's arms.

Serene said, "What happened out there? Who were those men who were trying to kill you?"

Indian said, "I stopped my horse because he was limping from something in his right front hoof, and as I was getting off I heard a bullet go over my head. A second shot hit my horse in the head and killed him.

"When he fell to the ground, I got behind his body and used it for a shield, and these two men kept shooting at me. I had bullets hitting all around me.

"After they fired several shots at me, the two men got on their horses and started riding down to where I was hiding behind my dead horse.

"By that time I had both of my pistols drawn and was waiting for them to get to my position.

"When they got there, I shot and killed both of them. Then I got their horses and rode to find you your river crossing and our campsite for the night.

"After I did that, I hightailed it back to find you, and here we are."

"So who were these men, and why were they trying to kill you?"

"It's a long story, but I'll keep it short. On the way to your ranch I was riding through Cedar City, Texas, and I was hungry and needed to get something to eat and drink.

"I was getting off my horse to go into a saloon when a man came running out of the saloon, yelling he was going to kill the first person he saw, and he fired a shot at me.

"He missed me, and I shot and killed him. People from the saloon told the local sheriff about this crazy kid saying he was going to kill the first person he saw as he was running out of the saloon. I turned out to be the first person he saw.

"The sheriff told me the kid had seven older brothers who would be trying to avenge their brother's death, and these two men were two of his brothers."

"You mean to tell me you have killed three brothers."

"No, actually, I've killed five of them. Two of them tried to kill me before I got to your ranch. There are still three brothers left."

"My God, Indian, I can't believe it. I've never heard of such a thing."

"Well, anyway, it's the truth. That's what happened. I wasn't trying to kill anybody. I'm just trying to stay alive!"

"Damn, don't you think the other brothers will come after you?"

"How in the hell should I know? I shouldn't have had to kill any of them. I was just trying to get something to eat and drink when this all started. I'd never been in Cedar City in my life. I never knew any of these people.

"You know the bartender who tried to kill me? It was because he was trying to get a reward from these people for killing me."

"My God, it gets worse as it goes. Who knows who's going to be gunning for you next? It could be anybody, maybe one of our own men."

"Serene, I don't think any of them would have any way of knowing about somebody paying a bounty to kill me."

"Oh no! These people could be hiring men to kill you all over Texas, and you wouldn't have any idea who they were. I don't think I can marry you. I don't want to be a widow before I can get back to my ranch."

"Serene, please don't say that. Please think about it before you make that decision, promise. Promise!

"Serene, I love you and want to marry you and spend our life together."

"OK, I'll think about it, really think about it before making a decision."

CHAPTER FOURTEEN

HELLO, OLD FRIEND, GLAD TO SEE YOU

THE NEXT MORNING, INDIAN skipped breakfast and took Miguel Cabrera and Carlos Espinal with him to help him bury the two men he had killed the day before.

Indian didn't want Serene to see what might be left of the two men's bodies after being left for the buzzards and coyotes all day and night. Indian wasn't sure what condition their bodies would be in, but he expected the worse.

When they arrived at the location of the bodies, their condition was worse than anything he could have imagined. The buzzards had made a good start on them, and the coyotes were still working on them.

Indian pulled out his rifle and killed one of the coyotes, and the other three ran off.

When Indian, Miguel, and Carlos arrived at the location of the bodies all three of them had to work hard to keep from throwing up after they saw the condition of the bodies. The bodies were missing eyes, and what was left of their internal organs were scattered all over the ground. Blood and pieces of flesh were everywhere.

The three men dug just one grave and placed whatever was left of the two men in it.

After they finished burying the men, Miguel and Carlos kneeled down beside the grave and made the sign of the cross.

Indian bowed his head and said, "Father, please take these men's souls into your loving care and forgive them of their sins. Amen."

Then the men headed back to the herd so they could help keeping the herd moving up the trail that Indian had planned for the trip to Dodge.

After catching up with the herd, Miguel and Carlos took up their positions for herding the cattle, and Indian rode off, searching for a location for their stop for the night.

*****

For the next few weeks, the cattle drive continued without many problems, and the routine was the same every day.

Things between Serene and Indian were still cool. Serene hadn't made up her mind about taking the chance of marrying Indian and winding up a widow before she could get back home.

She knew that two things were causing her big problems with her decision: she wanted him and she was in love with him, but she didn't want to be a widow!

They both went about their jobs without any conversation about anything except the job of moving the cattle up the trail, getting the men fed, crossing rivers, and pointing out locations of their campsites.

Today they would cross the Red River into Indian Territory and finally get out of Texas.

After finding a location suitable for crossing the Red River with the wagon and the cattle, Indian stopped across the river at a small trading post along the trail to see his old friend, Chuck Stone, who ran the trading post.

Going inside the trading post, Indian found Chuck, and after saying hello to him, Indian spotted someone in the trading post he never expected to find in this part of the country. It was a very dear friend he went to school with on the Cherokee Indian Reservation.

When Indian saw him, he said, "Hello, you old half-breed. What the hell are you doing way out here in the middle of nowhere?"

"None of your damn business, paleface!"

Indian opened both arms and reached out to his old friend.

His friend took Indian into his arms and lifted him off his feet. Indian was six foot two and over two hundred pounds, and his friend, Robert Smiley, was a mountain of a man who stood six foot seven and was three hundred plus pounds of solid muscle.

Robert's mother was a Cherokee Indian princess; her father was the chief of the Cherokees, and her grandfather was the great chief Sequoia, the man who developed the Cherokee Alphabet.

His father, Tom Smiley, was a white teacher from New York, and along with Robert's mother he taught at the missionary school that both he and Robert attended.

Robert's mother, White Dove, and Tom met when they both went to school somewhere back east, and they got married there without her parent's permission.

Robert told him his mother was almost banished from the tribe before her grandfather stood up for her. After he did, Tom was adopted into the tribe on the condition he continued to live on the reservation and teach at the missionary school.

Before Indian could ask, Robert told Indian that the last time he saw Indian's folks they were both well and were doing all right.

Indian asked, "Robert, what are you doing out here anyway?" Robert replied, "I'm on my way home after looking for gold in Colorado."

"Did you find a lot of gold?"

"About the same amount you found by not going to Colorado and not looking for it."

"That's not much." "Not much!"

"How about helping me move a herd of Longhorns up to Dodge?" "OK."

"Robert, there is one other little thing I need to tell you. It could be dangerous. I've got some people trying to kill me for defending myself when their brother tried to kill me."

"Oh, is that all? How bad are they trying?" "So far, I've had to kill five more men."

"That's a lot of bad! Man, they really want you dead, don't they?" "I think so!"

"OK, Indian, I'll try to help you stay on this side of the flower bed."

Indian said, "Robert, I have to ask you two questions. Are you still as good a shot with a rifle as you used to be, and do you still have that big bad Bowie knife you used to chase me around with?" "Don't worry, Indian. I can still hit whatever I aim at, and yes, I still have that knife and know how to use it."

"Good! Let's head out to the herd, and I'll introduce you to my boss."

Indian and Robert rode off to meet Indian's boss.

When they caught up with the chuck wagon, Serene and Granny were wondering what had happened to Indian since they thought they should be getting pretty close to the Red River and knew he would have to guide them across it.

Serene looked up and saw Indian and saw Robert with him and wondered if this was another bunch of Indians wanting cattle as payment for crossing their land.

She said to Indian, "Have we got a problem with another Indian tribe wanting to get paid for crossing their land?"

Robert tried to look as mean as he could and said, "Yes, ma'am, we want your whole damn herd!"

Indian couldn't help himself. He just started laughing, which caused Robert to start laughing too.

The only ones not in on the joke were Serene and Granny.

They just sat there in the wagon and looked first at Indian, then at Robert, and the longer they looked at them the more Indian and Robert laughed.

Finally, Indian said, "It's a joke, Serene. This is my best friend, Robert Smiley. We grew up together and went to school together. I've asked him to help us with the herd and help keep me alive."

Both the men got off their horses, and Indian said to Robert, "Robert, this is my boss, Serene Star, and her good friend and helper, Granny Hayes."

Serene smiled and said, "You're pretty funny, Robert. You really had me going there. I've never seen Indian laugh that much. Have you, Granny?"

"No, ma'am. I never did. I didn't know he knew how to laugh." Serene said, "I'm glad to have you with us and hope you can help us keep Indian alive. We need him to get my cattle to Dodge." "Ma'am, I'll do my best to help him and you."

"Good. Granny and I need to get to our campsite for the night and start fixing supper soon for the crew. I'll look forward to talking with you about what kind of kid Indian was growing up."

"Yes, ma'am. It'll be my pleasure."

Indian turned his horse and headed it back toward the Red River with Robert following right next to him.

After they were some distance ahead of the wagon, Robert said, "Wow! I didn't know a trail boss ever got a boss that looked like Serene."

"I never did before. Ain't she something Robert?" "I'd say she exquisite!"

"Where did you learn such a big word as 'exquisite'?"

"You know my dad and mom are both teachers, so I reckon some of their learning rubbed off on me."

"Yeah, I reckon just a little bit."

A few miles more and they reached the Red River, and Indian found his crossing place for the wagon and waited until Serene and

Granny arrived at the river; then he and Robert urged their horses to enter the river where Indian planned for the wagon to cross.

After they had the wagon safely across the river, Indian guided Serene to the location he chose for their campsite for the night.

Then Indian and Robert rode back to the herd and helped bring the herd to the river crossing and to that night's campsite.

On the way to find the herd Robert asked, "Indian, tell me about your boss lady."

"Not much to tell you except she was educated back east, and after she returned home to Texas for only a short time, her father was killed by rustlers. Her father had contacted me, asking me to bring a herd of Longhorns to Dodge. When I arrived at the ranch I found out her father had been killed, and she was the new owner of the ranch.

"She told me they had to get the cattle to market because her father had bought some more land to add on to the size of the ranch. They had a bank note due soon, and she didn't have enough money to pay off the loan and the bank was threatening to take her ranch if she couldn't pay off the note on time.

"I understand they had two herds stolen on the way to market earlier in the year, so this drive had to be made even though it is so late in the year.

"Robert, the one thing I haven't told you yet was I really fell for her and asked her to marry me when we got to Dodge.

"She agreed to marry me, but since I have all these people trying to kill me, she's kind of backed out. She doesn't want to be a widow."

"What do you mean, she's kind of backed out?"

"It means she has to think about it before committing to actually marrying me."

"Boy, Indian, you sure don't have a lot of luck in life, do you?"

"Sure I do. Don't I have you for my best friend? And Serene is at least thinking about marrying me. I think I'm pretty damn lucky, if you ask me."

"Well, you do have me for a faithful friend. I guess you are pretty lucky, not sure you're lucky enough to get that beautiful girl though!"

About that time they saw the herd coming up directly at them and quickly veered off to the right of the lead steers and soon joined in with the other drovers driving the herd.

Less than an hour later, they arrived at the Red River, and their campsite was just a short distance on the other side of the river.

The drovers began driving the herd directly into the river, and as soon as they crossed the river and they had enough room for the herd for the night, the drovers begin turning the herd to stop for the night.

This was always a tricky maneuver, turning the lead steers back toward the rest of the herd following them and getting them all to mill around until they finally stopped.

Tonight everything worked like magic: the river crossing and stopping the herd for the night.

Indian thought, "It should always work as easily as it did tonight."

CHAPTER FIFTEEN

THE REST OF THE TRIP TO DODGE SHOULD BE EASY

A S SOON AS THE cattle were bedded down for the night, Indian and Robert returned to the campsite.

When they arrived, Indian told Robert he would take care of their horses and took their horses over to the remuda so they both would have fresh mounts in the morning.

When Indian returned from taking the horses to the remuda, he found Serene at the back of the wagon, away from the campfire. They found, for once, they were alone, and Serene said, "Indian, you certainly got here fast. You must not have had many problems getting the herd across the Red River."

"No, Serene, the crossing and turning the herd was magic. Everything worked just like it is supposed to for once."

"I'm glad for that, and I'm glad your friend Robert was able to join us and certainly hope he can help keep you alive. How in the world did you come to find him in this part of the Territory?"

"I stopped at the trading post a few miles back from where we crossed the Red River to say hello to my old friend, Chuck Stone, who owns the trading post, and Robert was in the trading post on his way back home from Colorado where he had been looking for gold."

"Did Robert find any gold there?"

"No. I'm sorry he didn't. I asked him if he would come to help us with the herd and try to help keep me from getting killed. Robert is a crack shot and a mean man with a knife when he has to be."

"Indian, you know I love you, don't you?"

"I wasn't sure you still did. I know I love you so much and want to marry you as soon as we get to Dodge. I want to spend the rest of my life with you."

"OK, well, I thought about it a lot, and I would rather marry you and be with you for only one day than to never have you. I want to marry you."

Indian reached for Serene and took her in his arm and softly kissed her lips, and then he pulled her closer and kissed her harder.

Suddenly they heard a familiar voice say, "Serene, I need you to help me finish supper."

It was Granny Hayes, who always seemed to show up every time the two of them were alone.

Serene pulled herself out of Indian's arms and said, "Yeah, Granny. I'll be right there."

She added, "Indian, I've got to help Granny with supper, but you've got a date. We'll be married in Dodge as soon as we get rid of the herd."

Serene turned to go back to help fix supper for the drovers. All Indian could do was stand there and smile.

What he wanted to do was to whisk away the herd and marry Serene right then.

What he did do was to go check on the crew to make sure everyone was doing all right and no one was having a problem. He wanted to be sure they could move the Longhorns across Indian Territory as quickly as possible and up to Dodge before many more weeks passed.

Indian was still afraid of the weather this time of the year. He knew any day could produce a winter storm that could kill off half the herd and maybe some of the drovers as well.

He had never taken a herd of Longhorns on a drive this late in the year and for the number of miles this drive was. Most of the ranches he worked for were located in central Texas.

The Star Ranch was many more miles farther east and south than where his regular cattle drives started.

He knew he couldn't lose Serene's herd and let her lose her ranch. Her father had spent his life building a ranch as large as the Star Ranch, and she would never forgive herself if they weren't successful in getting the herd to Dodge and getting back to Texas to pay off the bank loan on time.

Indian planned to move the herd additional miles every day from now on and had to hope his crew and the cattle could take it.

After supper, Indian introduced Robert to the crew and told them Robert was his best friend and they had gone to school together. Then he told them that he planned on going at least twenty miles every day from now until they got to Dodge.

This meant they would be in the saddle for two more hours a day than the ten hours a day they had been riding. Indian heard a few groans out of his men, and he said, "Remember, we need to get the herd to Dodge before December 10 to get the herd shipped out. "If we make that date without losing any more than hundred steers, there will be an additional bonus of sixty dollars per man." Then the groans turned into "Yippee!"

After Indian made his talk to the crew, he searched Serene out to tell her what he had just promised the men and to let her and Granny know they were going to have to get up even earlier and stay up even later than they had been if they were going to make it to Dodge before the tenth of December.

Indian said, "Serene, we have about two hundred and fifty miles to go from here to Dodge, and if we make twenty miles a day, then we could get there in about thirteen days. But if we have any kind of big problem, we might not be able to make it to Dodge by the tenth of December.

"Right now we have twenty days to make it, but I don't want to take any chances that something really big and bad happens on the drive, and we wouldn't have time to recover without having extra days built into our schedule. I want to give us a cushion just in case someone or something stampedes the herd and it takes us three or four days to round them up.

"I'm also giving away more of your money. I just promised the crew we would pay each of them an extra sixty dollars bonus if we got to Dodge by December 10 and if we didn't lose more than a hundred steers.

"I hope that's OK with you. We need to keep the men happy and keep them motivated to get the job done, and having them in the saddle two more hours a day is going to be tough on them.

"It's not going to be any picnic for you and Granny either, putting in even more hours every day. I'm sorry we have to do it, but I don't think we can take chances of not making it to Dodge on time. Sorry."

"Indian, you are running this drive. Everyone will have to do whatever you think has to be done to make it to Dodge on time to get the cattle to market. I wish you had told me you thought we needed to give the crew a bigger bonus before you did it, but I don't have a problem with it."

"OK, Serene. I'll check with you on things before I spend any more of your money."

Serene smiled and thought, "No, he probably won't because he was too used to being in charge of whatever he did." In a way, she really liked having a man who took charge.

Serene said, "So, you're telling me that starting tomorrow morning, Granny and I need to get up an hour earlier than what we've been doing, right?"

"Right."

"You know, Indian, I think you might have a mean streak in you."

"Serene, how can you say that? I'm just telling everyone what has to be done to be sure you have the money to pay off your loan and let you keep your ranch."

Serene didn't reply she just came up very close to Indian. He took her in his arms and gave her a very tender kiss and said, "I love you, Boss lady."

"I love you too, cowboy, more than you probably love me." "Why would you say that, Serene?"

"My mommy told me about cowboys when I was a little girl. She told me never to fall in love with a cowboy because they will love you and leave you. Is that what you're going to do?"

"Serene, I'll never leave you until the good Lord calls me home. I love you way too much to even think about leaving you."

With that, Indian kissed her with much more passion than before, and when the kiss was over, they both were left wanting a lot more than kisses.

Serene said, "Indian, I've got to go. I have to cool off before I get into the wagon to go to bed. Wow, I never felt this before. I really want you."

"I understand. You're not by yourself. I never experienced anything like the feeling I had after that kiss. Thinking about what I feel right now, it's going to be a really hard time these next twenty days before we can get married in Dodge. Whew! Tough, baby, tough!"

Serene slowly turned back in the direction of the wagon and told herself, "OK, Serene, you can do it. Just take one small step at a time and don't look back at Indian, or you be flying back into his arms."

She continued thinking, "Cattle, ranch, what the hell!" She would rather have Indian right now than anything else in this world.

She thought it was a good thing it was dark because she wouldn't want anyone to see her face right now; it was burning with desire.

Serene stopped at the water barrel and took a slow drink of water and then washed her face with it; even though the water wasn't cool, it did help a little. She didn't feel quite so flushed.

When she managed to climb up into the wagon, Granny said, "Where have you been, child? I was getting worried about you."

"Sorry, Granny. I was talking with Indian, who was telling me we had to get up an hour earlier to get breakfast because he said we need to be traveling another two hours a day to be sure we make it to Dodge before the tenth of December to be able to ship out the steers."

"Well, Serene, I reckon we'll have to learn to sleep fast if we are going to be getting up an hour earlier, which also means we're going to be going to bed an hour later. Damn, cowboys got it easy. All they have to do is ride another couple of hours every day."

"Granny, I don't think they're going to think so since they still have to ride night guard as well."

"Good night, child. We'll do what we have to do." "Good night, Granny."

Indian was having his own problem going to his bedroll and trying to get some sleep.

All he could do was think about Serene and how much he wanted to marry her and make love with her and be with her every moment. To him, nothing else mattered anymore.

He did have a few problems he had to take care of first: getting three thousand head of Longhorns to Dodge before December 10; making sure all his crew made it safely to Dodge and back home; staying alive while a whole bunch of people were trying to kill him; helping Serene sell the cattle and collect the money; and getting Serene and the money back to Cuero, Texas, to pay off the loan before the bank foreclosed on the ranch.

He guessed that was about all he had to do besides marry Serene as soon as they got to Dodge.

*****

103

Serene heard Granny say, "Serene, honey, it's time for us to get up to fix breakfast."

"What time is it, Granny?" "It's 4:00 a.m."

"OK, I'm getting up."

Hearing that, Granny climbed down out of the wagon and restarted the fire and put on a pot of coffee, the first of many pots to make that day, she was sure.

True to her word, Serene was out of the wagon and began working on putting together the ingredients to make biscuits. She knew they were going to need extra biscuits every day from now on to keep the drovers awake and riding.

Doing without enough sleep, Serene thought the crew was going to have to have extra food to make up for the lack of sleep. Maybe she was wrong, but she always thought she had to have something extra to eat when she didn't get enough sleep, so her drovers probably would too.

In the meantime, Granny was putting on a big pot of beans and getting ready to fry up the last of their bacon. It looked like from now on the drovers would have to make do with hardtack for their long days in the saddle.

Indian had been up for some time and had already been out to check on the night herders and was just riding back to the campsite when he saw a group of riders coming toward the campsite, riding fast.

Indian quickly reined his horse so he was headed directly at the riders. He kicked his steed in the side to get him on a dead run to try to reach the riders before they reached the campsite.

The lead rider saw Indian racing toward them and pulled his horse up, and the rest of the riders did the same.

Indian pulled his horse up and brought him to a halt. Indian dove out of his saddle and at the same time pulled his rifle out of its scabbard.

Indian called out to the riders, "What do you men want?"

One of the men replied, "We're looking for a man named Indian Leader. We heard he's a trail boss riding this way with a herd of Longhorns."

"Why are you looking for him?"

"We heard he was bringing in a herd to Dodge, and we thought he might need some help."

"I'm Leader, and we don't need any more help."

The same man who had been talking replied, "We would really like to talk with you because we heard some talk in Dodge about you going to be riding into some big trouble. Some rancher from Texas was saying you killed his brother, and he and his men are waiting for you and you would never make it to Dodge alive and neither would your herd. They are going to bushwhack you a few miles from Dodge."

"OK, you come on down here to where I'm at, and let's talk about what you think you can do to help me, just you. The rest of the men with you are to stay where they're at."

"OK, I'll be right there."

The lead rider in the group of men slowly started his horse forward, riding to where Indian was standing by his horse. The rest of the men stayed where they had stopped.

When the rider got to where Indian could see him clearly, Indian could see the man looked like he was pretty down on his luck and could really use a job.

Indian said, "OK, you can get off your horse but do it slowly so I can see your every move."

The man slowly stepped down from his horse and turned to face Indian and said, "We don't mean you any harm. We're trying to get back home to Texas, and we lost all the money in Dodge City we made taking a herd to Wyoming. There's a gambler there who's real good at poker, or he's real good at getting good hands. Anyway, he won all our money, and we've been trying to find work to make enough to help us get home."

"Do you know the name of this gambler?"

"Well, some of the men with him called him Mr. Eagle, but I'm not sure it's his name." "Why do you say that?"

"Cause a fellow at the bar told me after we lost all our money that the guy was called Black Jack Eagle, a gambler from St. Louis, known to kill several people who thought he was cheating. I guess he's really fast on the draw."

"That same fellow who told you that, is he the one who told you some people were in Dodge waiting to kill me?"

"Yeah, he was."

"So how did he know, or did he say who it was who was trying to kill me?"

"Yeah. He said he was one of the men waiting for you along with his boss, Sam Phillips. I think that's what he said his boss's name was."

"What's your name, cowboy?"

"Charles Webster."

"How many men are with you, Charles?" "Four."

"The best I can do is to pay each of you $30 and a bonus of $10 if we get the cattle to Dodge before December 10."

"Mr. Leader, I can tell you we sure appreciate it, and we'll do a good job for you."

"OK, you go back and tell the other fellows with you that they got a job but they're going to be riding twelve hours a day until we get to Dodge."

"Thanks. I'll go tell them."

"You can also tell them breakfast will be ready when they get up to the campsite."

"Thanks. They're going to be happy to hear that because we haven't had anything to eat for a couple of days."

Charles rode off to tell his friends they had jobs and breakfast would be ready for them when they got to the campsite.

Indian rode back to tell Serene he had just spent another $200 of her money, and he wasn't looking forward to doing that either.

CHAPTER SIXTEEN

THE HARD PUSH TO DODGE

INDIAN RODE BACK TO the campsite and told Serene they needed to talk right away. She told him OK.

Indian reached out his hand to Serene and took his foot out of the stirrup. Serene took his hand and placed her foot in the stirrup and Indian pulled her up behind him.

Serene put her arms around him and said, "Granny, I got to go talk with Indian for a while."

Indian added, "Granny, there are five hungry men riding into camp and please feed them breakfast. Thanks."

Indian rode off with Serene, her arms around him.

After riding a short way, Indian stopped his horse and asked Serene to get off. She did as he asked, and Indian got off right after her.

Indian started the conversation by saying, "Serene, I've got a lot of bad news. First, I just hired five more cowboys to help us get to Dodge, so I'm spending another $200 of your money."

Serene replied, "Well, that's not the worst thing you could tell me."

"No, it's not. The rest of the news is that one of the Phillips brothers and his men are waiting in Dodge to kill me."

"That's bad news."

"It gets worse. Your wonderful neighbor, Mr. Kent Eagle, is also waiting in Dodge for us to get there."

"How did you find out all of this?"

"One of the men I just hired to help us told me about it. It seems one of the Phillips hired gunman told him they were in Dodge to kill me.

"Plus, Mr. Eagle has resumed his old profession, gambling. He won all the money the five cowboys earned from taking a herd up to Wyoming. That's why the cowboys came looking for me to see if they could help us and earn enough money to get back home in Texas."

"Indian, do you trust what they told you is true?"

"Yes, I do. Why do I believe them? I didn't tell you. I saw your Mr. Eagle in town when I was sending telegraphs to the cattle buyers and recognized him from my old job before becoming a trail boss."

"What job did you have?"

"I was a deputy sheriff for St. Louis County, Missouri, and we had several run-ins with Mr. Eagle, who was called Black Jack Eagle in St. Louis. He was involved in several killings but always had lots of witnesses that it was self-defense, so we could never hang him."

"How did you get to be a deputy sheriff in St. Louis?"

"I saved the sheriff's life one night when I was taking a walk by the Mississippi River. I had been a cowboy and wanted to go see the biggest city in the west. Next thing I knew I was a deputy sheriff.

"I left the job because I was getting too much of a reputation as a fast-draw lawman, and I didn't want to be drawn into gunfights and have to kill every gunslinger in the west wanting to make a reputation for himself. So now I'm in this mess killing people every other day it seems like."

"Indian, I'm so sorry you got into this mess trying to help my father and me."

"Serene, I think Black Jack Eagle either killed your father or had one of his men kill him. He's the one who's behind rustling your cattle and the one who stole your two herds on the way to market. I'm sure he either won or stole the ranch next to you.

"You said he wanted to marry you, and I can tell you what he wants is your ranch and he is willing to do whatever it takes to get it. If he could get you for his wife, it would make everything just that much sweeter.

"Serene, Black Jack Eagle is as bad as they come. While working as a deputy, I saw a lot of bad hombres, and he's as bad as any of them and slicker than all the ones we put in prison or hung." "Indian, why didn't you tell me before about what you knew about Kent Eagle?"

"I tried never to let anyone know I served as a deputy. When I was made a deputy in St. Louis, I used a different name so I wouldn't have my reputation as a lawman follow me all my life. I called myself Johnny Able."

"OK, Indian, or Johnny, or whatever your name is, I love you just the same."

"Serene, since I'm telling you about myself, I have to tell you the entire story of my life. I was born in Indian Territory, and my father and mother were killed by Indians. The man who raised me as his son was a Cherokee Indian. He and his wife became my mother and father. He found me when I was about four years old wandering around not very far from where we are right now.

"The only things I had were the clothes on my back, and I was carrying a Bible. In the Bible my mother had written I was born in Indian Territory, so she named me 'Indian.' I went to school on the reservation with my best friend, Robert Smiley. His mother was a Cherokee princess, and his father was a white man from back east, and they met when they were both going to college somewhere in the east and got married.

"They became teachers on the reservation, where Robert was born. We both had them for our teachers.

"After I was old enough, I left home to become a real cowboy and worked at every job there was being a cowboy, including going on lots of trail jobs.

"That's probably enough information on my life to let you off the hook so you don't have to marry me."

"I only have one question, Indian. Are your father and mother still living on the reservation, and do you ever see them?"

"Yes. Robert told me the last time he saw them they were both doing well and still living on the reservation. I try to go see them at least once a year."

"Good! I'd like to meet them one day."

"I would really like for them to meet you and show them what a wonderful woman I found."

"Then, cowboy, we better get this herd to Dodge. I guess you're going to have to kill whoever is standing in our way of getting married. If that's what it's going to take to marry you, do it."

Without another word Indian put his foot in the stirrup and rose up gracefully into his saddle and then reached for Serene's hand and pulled her up behind him.

Before they were back at the campsite Serene said, "Indian, we're going to have to buy more supplies with the extra men we have."

"OK, Serene, as soon as you have the men fed, we'll make a trip to Chuck Stone's Trading Post before we get too far away since there's nothing else between here and Dodge to buy any kind of supplies.

By the time Indian and Serene returned to the campsite, Granny had all the men fed and was loading up the chuck wagon to get ready to push on for the day. The drovers had all left the campsite and were already moving out the herd.

Indian dropped Serene off to help Granny get the chuck wagon ready to move out while he rode to the herd and found his point men had already assigned the five new men to positions along the herd. Indian thought they were good men, because they already had the herd moving.

When Indian realized he didn't see Robert, he asked if the point men knew where he was, and before they could answer, Robert rode up behind him.

Robert said, "Good morning, Boss, don't worry. I've been trailing along behind you since you first rode out this morning."

"I sure didn't see you."

"It's OK. I saw you talking to one of the men from the group of five and saw you ride to the campsite and pick up Serene and take her away from the campsite and hold a long conversation with her then take her back to the campsite, and then I followed you here."

"Damn, Robert, I must be slipping. I never saw or heard you."

"It's OK, paleface. Your Indian is looking out for you."

"That's good. Let's go back to the campsite. We're going to have to go pick up more supplies back at Chuck Stone's Trading Post since we got six more mouths to feed now, including one with a really big mouth."

"Ugh, we go."

"What happened to that exquisite conversationalist I was riding with yesterday?"

"Ugh, me just dumb Indian now."

"Just why are you a dumb Indian now?"

"I don't want anyone to think I understand English too well. Sometimes, when people are around Indians and think they don't know much English, they will say too much about the wrong thing. "If we are around people who don't know us, I might have a chance to hear things they wouldn't want you to know, and when we're out on the trail I will be following you to make sure nobody else is. Do you understand now?"

"I understand you're pretty damn smart, Robert." "Well, I'd better be if I'm going to help keep you alive."

On arriving back at the campsite, Indian found Serene and Granny had finished loading the chuck wagon and were hitching up the team.

Indian asked, "Do you want to go shopping, Boss lady?"

"I sure do. I think we're going to need a lot more supplies if you keep hiring cowboys."

When Serene and Granny were in the wagon, Serene said, "Let's go buy out the trading post."

111

Indian rode beside the wagon and Robert was now nowhere in sight.

"Where did Robert go?" Serene asked.

"He's staying out of sight so he can watch out for me better than being right beside me. It was his idea, and I think it's a good one."

"Sounds like it could be."

On arriving at the trading post, Indian introduced Serene and Granny to Chuck Stone, the owner of the trading post, and by the time they gave Chuck their order for all the things they needed, Chuck had become a good friend to all of them.

Indian always thought Chuck was a very good man and had a good business and took good care of his customers. He normally closed the trading post this time a year and went to Dodge City to buy his supplies to restock his trading post. Before the railroad made it to Dodge, he would go all the way to Kansa City to restock his store.

Chuck said he might catch up with them when they arrived in Dodge. Serene invited him to come to their wedding if he was still in town. He said he was normally there for a couple of months and would be honored to come to their wedding.

Indian escorted the women back to the trail, and when he had them ahead of the herd, he told Serene, "Just keep on a straight line headed north, and you'll be in Dodge someday."

Indian rode on to check out the trail and to locate a place for their campsite tonight. It didn't take him long to find a campsite, and then he pushed on for several more miles to check out how the trail looked ahead. He was surprised that this late in the year there seemed to be some green grass still growing. Indian never expected to see that.

He turned his horse around and urged his horse into a trot and headed back to find Serene and the chuck wagon. It was several hours before he spotted the chuck wagon, and after he met the wagon, he told Serene, "I found you a nice campsite for the night. It's got some water and some grass for the cattle."

After telling Serene where to look for their campsite that night, he rode back to catch up with the herd and stayed with Alex. He told Alex he wanted him to be in charge of the herd if he wasn't with them, and if something happened to Alex, then Miguel would take charge.

Alex was surprised that Indian wanted him to be in charge of the herd if anything happened to him or if he was away from the herd.

Indian told Alex he would have a meeting tonight with the crew to tell them if he wasn't with the herd, Alex was in charge of the drive.

After they reached the campsite for the night and the herd was bedded down and as the drovers were having their dinner, Indian announced to all the crew that if he was absent from the drive, Alex Gonzales would take over as trail boss, and if something happened to Alex, then Miguel Cabrera would assume the responsibility of being the trail boss.

After dinner, Indian told Serene they needed to sign up the new men in her payroll book.

Serene got her payroll book from the wagon and took down the names of the five new men: Charles Webster, Bob Perry, John Napier, Tom Elliott, and Ron Brown.

She also added Robert Smiley to her payroll book and wondered where he was since he hadn't come in for supper with the rest of the men.

They wouldn't see Robert for several days after that, but Indian was sure he wasn't far away from him, no matter where he was.

Day after day the drovers pushed the herd toward Dodge at least twelve hours a day, and Indian pushed everyone to keep doing it.

Tempers were getting short. Even Serene snapped back at some of the drovers when they asked for extra coffee.

It seemed Granny and Indian were the only two who just kept their heads bowed down and kept doing their job.

After ten days of moving the herd at least twenty miles a day, Indian announced at supper, "We are only a few days out of Dodge, and since we have good water and some grass here, we're stopping for a couple of days to let the cattle get some rest and everyone else can get some rest too."

Everyone was shocked at the announcement, but they were happy to have a chance to rest and let the cattle have time to rest and eat.

Later that evening, Serene told Indian, "I'm glad you decided to let the men and cattle get some rest. I know they're tired, and so am I. It's been a hard trip, a lot harder than I could have ever imagined."

"Serene, I'm sorry you had to make the trip, and I want you to know how much I admire you for doing it. You're a treasure, and I love you."

"Indian, I have no idea how you have made so many of these trips. They're awful."

"Doing trail drives has been my life for a lot of years. I love the fact that I feel very proud of the men who rode with me, and accomplishing something great when the drive is over gives me a great feeling."

"You deserve to feel great about finishing these drives. Even though I don't ever want to do another one, I feel proud to be a part of one drive."

"Serene, we're not quite finished, but we'll make it right on time and you'll be able to get your cattle sold and get back in time to pay off your note.

"The other reason I wanted to stop the drive here is I plan to ride on in to Dodge and let the buyers know we'll have the herd in Dodge in about three days. While I'm in Dodge, I'll see if I can't do something with the Phillips brothers. Maybe I can get lucky and talk them into going home and forgetting about me."

"Indian, do you really think that's going to happen after killing five of them?"

"No, but I wish it would."

"What about Kent Eagle and his men?"

"I'll try to avoid him if there is any way possible until after we get the cattle sold."

"When are you leaving for Dodge?" "First thing in the morning."

"Darling, be careful. Don't let the man I love get himself killed or anything like that."

"OK, I'll try to do that."

Indian took Serene into his arms and began kissing her and holding her body close to his, and he began to feel a great desire for her.

He stopped the kisses and released her from his arms and said, "Serene, I have to stop. I'm afraid I can't keep from making love to you right now if we don't. I want the first time we make love to be special and in someplace special, not out here in on the prairie."

"I don't want you to stop. I need you right now."

Indian reached for her and pulled her close to him again and began kissing her, when he heard a horse coming up behind them.

Indian stopped, released Serene from his arms, and turned in the direction of the sound of a horse's hoofs. He drew his gun and waited for whoever was coming up to them.

Robert said, "Indian, is that you and Serene?" "Yeah, it us."

"Sure hope I'm not interrupting anything."

"No, Robert, I was just telling Serene I was going into Dodge tomorrow to see if I could talk the Phillips brothers into going home and forgetting about me."

Robert was pretty sure there was a lot more going on, but he wasn't going to push it.

"So what time are we leaving to go to Dodge?" "Right after we have breakfast."

"Sounds good to me. See you both in the morning."

Robert turned his horse back toward the campsite and said, "Good night."

Indian and Serene began walking back to the campsite hand in hand, and Serene said, "Indian, whenever we make love the first time it will be special wherever we are, and it will always be special every time."

CHAPTER SEVENTEEN

WELCOME TO DODGE CITY

NDIAN AND ROBERT WERE in their saddles and on their way to Dodge very early the next morning. Robert said "Indian, when we get close to Dodge, I will go into town ahead of you so people don't know we are together."

"Good idea. I wouldn't want you to get shot by being next to me."

"Right. That's just what I meant. I don't want people shooting at you and hitting me."

"Yeah, I know how you are. I remember when we were little and three bigger boys were beating up on me and you just stood there watching them for a long time before you helped me. Yeah, I remember."

"Hell, Indian, there were only three of them, and I thought you wouldn't need any help."

"I'm glad you did finally decide to help since the three of them were doing a pretty good job on me until you stepped in."

"Yes, and then what happened? Your father came up when we were whipping their butts, and he stopped the fight and gave both of us a whipping for beating up on those poor boys."

"Robert, I guess that should prove to you that you can't win when you try to help me."

"So what in the hell am I doing here now?"

"Damned if I know! Guess you ain't as smart as I thought you were."

"I think you're right. I'm sure not very smart to get involved with your fights, so guess I better get on my way."

Robert put his horse in gallop and left Indian behind him.

Indian just smiled and thought, "It's hard to ever get a friend as loyal as Robert." He was lucky to have him.

When Indian arrived in Dodge, he went directly to the offices of the cattle buyers and told all three of them that the three thousand head of Longhorns would be delivered to Dodge in three days.

All three of the buyers were interested in buying the herd. Indian told them he would be back in about an hour and he needed their bid for the herd then.

Indian made his way over to the Dodge House and had lunch in their dining room.

After he finished lunch, Indian went back to the cattle buyers to get their bid and told them as soon as he had all three of their bids he would tell them who had the winning bid on the cattle.

After he made the rounds to the three cattle buyers, he saw that the bid from Mr. Greenback was the highest bid, at $35.75 per animal.

Indian made his way back to the two buyers who had the losing bids and let them know that the Chicago Cattle Company was buying their herd for $35.75 for each animal.

Then he went back to let Mr. Greenback know he had won the bid. Indian told him he needed to be paid in cash when the cattle were delivered to the railroad pens. He told Mr. Greenback that as far as he knew, they had slightly over three thousand head of cattle coming in.

Greenback said he would be ready to pay for the cattle in cash when the herd was put into the railroad cattle pens. Indian thanked him and then went looking for the Phillips brothers.

Indian went over to the Long Branch Saloon to get a drink and see who might be in the saloon, and to see if he could spot either the Phillips bunch or the Eagle outlaws. He thought if he didn't say too much, he might be able to see if either of the two groups was hanging around in the saloon.

He cautiously made his way into the Long Branch, found a table at the back of the saloon, and ordered a bottle of whiskey.

After being out in the bright sunlight, Indian found it hard to see in the dark saloon.

After his eyes became more accustomed to the darkened room, he could see several men over at one table playing poker and a couple of men sitting at the bar talking with the bartender.

One thing he knew: Black Jack Eagle wasn't involved in the poker game, and he didn't recognize the two men at the bar.

After sitting there for some time, a barroom girl came down from upstairs and looked around the saloon and made her way over to Indian's table.

After seeing who he was, she sat down at the table and said softly, "Indian, you may not know who I am, but I know you from when you came into the bar to buy drinks for your men. My name is Wanda, and I need to tell you some things."

"Wanda, would you like a drink?" "Sure, I need one."

"What do you want to drink?

"Whatever you have in that bottle will do."

Indian asked the bartender to bring Wanda a glass, and he promptly brought her one.

"Indian, the two guys sitting at the bar are waiting for you. They say they're here to kill you."

"Do you know their names?"

"Not really, I only know they work for a man named Sam Phillips."

"Is Sam Phillips here now?"

"No. He's upstairs in his room. I saw him go into his room when I went up to my room about thirty minutes ago."

"What room is he in?"

"It's at the top of the stairs, number 12." "Can you go upstairs with me right now?" "Sure I can, if you think it will help."

"I think it might save some lives." "OK, let's go."

"First, I have to pay for this bottle, and we'll take it upstairs with us like we're going to have ourselves a party."

"Swell, I love parties."

Indian asked the bartender how much he owed him for the bottle and was told it was $4.00. Indian paid him, and then Wanda and Indian made their way up the stairs.

When they got to the top of the stairs, Indian asked Wanda to knock on the door and tell Mr. Phillips she had a bottle of whiskey that a friend sent up to him.

Wanda did as she was asked, and when Mr. Phillips opened the door, Indian held a gun pointed directly at Sam Phillips's head.

Indian and Wanda pushed their way into Mr. Phillips's room, and Indian told him to sit down on the bed because he wanted to talk to him.

Since Indian continued to have his .44 Colt pointed directly at Mr. Phillips's face, he did as he was told and sat down on the bed.

After Wanda closed the door, Indian put his Colt back into its holster and said, "You are Sam Phillips, aren't you?"

"Yeah, I'm Sam Phillips."

"Sam, I'm Indian Leader, and I want to get something straightened out with you and your brother right now. I've been trying to do it for some time now, and instead of having any of the Phillips listen to me, I've had to kill them to stay alive myself.

"I don't know what you think I've done, but I want you to know I don't have anything against you or your brothers. I never even heard of the Phillips brothers until one night several months ago I was getting off my horse to go into a saloon to have something to eat and drink when some man came out of that saloon yelling, 'I'm going to kill the first person I see.'

"The next thing I heard was a bullet whistling by my ear, and I pulled my gun and shot the man shooting at me.

"So far, I've had to kill four more of your brothers and a bartender who was trying to kill me for whatever you folks were offering to pay people to kill me.

"It's time we stopped these useless killings caused by a drunken young man who was trying to kill the first person he saw, and I'm sorry to say it was me.

"Here's the deal: you can call off your men and the reward you're offering people to kill me. Get on your horses and go back home and make it the end of this or I'm going to kill you, and then, as soon as I finish delivering this herd of cattle to Dodge, I'm going to go back to Cedar City, Texas, find your brother, and kill him.

"One last part of the deal is if anyone else tries to kill me over this and I kill them, I'll be getting on my horse and heading directly to Cedar City to kill you and your brother. Am I making it clear enough? The killing is over between the Phillips and me.

"Let's have a drink, and you can think it over and let me know your answer after you finish your drink. In case you think you can outdraw me, let me show you something."

Before Indian finished saying it, his gun was in his hand pointed directly at Sam Phillips's ample belly.

Wanda poured drinks out for the three of them in the water glasses she found in the room.

Then she handed one glass to Sam Phillips and one glass to Indian; she took the third one for herself and took a deep breath.

Indian put his gun back in its holster and took a drink.

Sam Phillips had said nothing so far; he did take a big drink of the whiskey and took a deep breath.

Indian said, "One other thing, Sam, Wanda here had nothing to do with this. I made her do it, and if I hear that you or one of your men laid a finger on her, they will be answering to me with their lives. Got that?"

Sam finished his glass of whiskey and said, "Indian, I think you're right. We've lost enough of our family, so I agree to take my men and go back to Texas, and it's the end of this whole affair.

"I'm sorry we caused you so many problems and am really sorry for the loss of so many of my brothers.

"Phillips is a proud family, and we have never let anybody get away with anything against us our whole lives. But I do agree that our family has paid too big a price to try to avenge the loss of our youngest brother. My men and I will be leaving town tonight."

Indian put out his right hand to shake Sam's hand, and Sam hesitated for a second, thinking he could probably pull his gun and kill Indian before he could reach his gun with his hand sticking out in the air waiting for Sam to shake it.

But Indian said, "Sam, don't try it."

It was if Indian could read Sam's mind.

Instead of reaching for his gun, he took Indian's hand and said, "It's a deal."

"Good. Before you go, I have some things in my saddlebags that belonged to your brothers that I had planned to send to you when I got somewhere to mail them."

"That would be nice of you."

"I'll go down to my horse and bring the items to you."

Indian and Wanda left Sam's room to go back downstairs so Indian could go out to his horse and get the items for Sam to take back home.

Indian dug the items out of his saddlebags and took them upstairs and knocked on Sam's door. Indian stood away from the door in case Sam had a change of heart, but Sam opened the door, and Indian went inside the room with the items for Sam.

Sam had been packing his things, getting ready to leave as he said he would. Then Indian laid almost five hundred dollars on the bed and the two gold pocket watches he had taken off the bodies of Sam's brothers.

Sam couldn't believe how honest Indian was to give him back almost five hundred dollars and two very expensive gold pocket watches.

Sam thanked him again and walked down the stairs with Indian and told his two men, who were sitting at the bar, they were going back to Texas. Both of the men got up from the bar without asking any questions and went with Sam out the door.

Indian followed them out to their horses, and before Sam got on his horse, he shook Indian's hand again and wished him well.

"Sam, I'm truly sorry about your brothers, but they didn't give me any choice. I want you take this bottle of whiskey so you have a little something to keep you warm on your ride home.

Sam got on his horse, and the two men with him rode off, out of Dodge.

Indian was hoping that was the end of the Phillips brothers trying to kill him.

What Indian didn't know was that other people in Dodge also recognized him and told Kent Eagle he was in town, so Kent knew Serene Star's herd must be pretty close. It was time to make his move.

Kent decided the best thing he could do was let Serene sell her herd and then steal the money before she left Dodge.

He figured that way she couldn't pay off her mortgage. Then he could buy her ranch with her own money and for less than what she owed on the mortgage.

He thought it was a good plan. It was better than stealing her herd like he had twice already this year. "Hell, let them do the work of getting the damn cattle to Dodge. It would be a helluva lot easier than pushing a herd of Longhorns up the trail."

Yeah, he liked the idea a lot, and he figured that when she didn't have a ranch, she would reconsider his marriage offer. He really wanted that woman; she was like no woman he had ever had, and she was a lady, and almost as smart as he was.

After thinking his plan over again, he decided maybe it would be better if he kidnapped her. That way he knew she couldn't get the money to pay off the loan. If she wasn't in Cuero when the note was due, she couldn't pay off the note.

One big problem was he didn't think she would marry him if he kidnapped her, or if she did, one day she would figure out a way to kill him.

No, he would have to have some of his men kidnap her, and he needed to get back to Texas to be sure she never thought he had anything to do with it.

Kent called his two most trusted men into his bedroom, Al Beckett and Lightning Cole.

Kent said, "Al, I want you and Lightning to kidnap Serene Star and take her to Kansas City and keep her there until you hear from me. Whatever you do, you don't hurt her and you don't molest her in any way, or I'll kill you. You both understand my meaning, don't you?"

Both men nodded they understood.

Lightning asked, "When do you want us to get her?"

"I think it would be better if you grabbed her before she gets to Dodge. I understand she is doing the cooking for the cattle drive along with an old lady they call Granny something. So it should be easy to get her when the chuck wagon is away from the herd.

"One more thing, you want to be sure that trail boss is not around. I understand he's fast on the draw. I don't want to take any chances she might get hit in a gunfight."

Al asked, "OK, Boss, but how do we know what she looks like?"

"Al, there's only two women on the chuck wagon, and one of them is called Granny. So I think when you see them, you won't have much trouble figuring out which one is Serene Star. She's a beautiful young woman. I expect her to be my wife when this is all over.

"To be sure she doesn't suspect I'm involved in any way, I want you to talk about how smart your boss, Indian, is. You tell her you're not going to hurt her, and you'll set free her as soon as your boss lets you know when she can go. Got it?"

Both of the men replied, "Got it."

Kent gave the two men five hundred dollars to buy train tickets, food, and lodging in Kansas City for the three of them.

Kent said, "You do this right, and I'll pay you $1,000 a piece when I come to get the girl. You can contact me by telegraph in Texas to let me know where I can find you after you get to Kansas City, OK?

Lightning replied, "You got it, Boss. One more thing: to take the train, we'll have to take her over to the next stop east of Dodge. I think it's a town they call Hutchinson."

"Well, you might be able to flag down the east-bound train since you'll have your sister with you. Turn loose a couple of your horses and tell them you got jumped by some Indians and they took your horses."

"Good idea, Boss. That would save us more than hundred miles of riding, but it might be pretty hard to keep the woman from talking on the train ride."

"Tell the conductor your sister is crazy, and you're taking her to a doctor in Kansas City to see if he can help her. You tell him she keeps telling people you're kidnapping her and acts like she doesn't know who you are. You tell the man sometimes you have to restrain her to keep her from hurting herself or somebody else."

"Boss, you've got an answer for everything. Guess we better get going."

Lightning and Al left Kent's room, gathered up their stuff, and left Dodge to find Serene.

Kent was pleased he had men like Al and Lightning working for him. Al had worked for him a long time and would do anything he asked him. Lightning had not been working for him too long, but he was a top man with either a six-shooter or a rifle.

Lightning got his nickname because he drew a gun like a lightning flash—quick and deadly.

Kent didn't know how many men Lightning had killed, but he had killed three men for him already.

Lightning was kind of like an attack dog; all Kent had to do was point his finger and say "Get him," and it was done.

Kent thought he better get out of Dodge before Indian saw him; besides, it was a long ride back to Texas.

CHAPTER EIGHTEEN

THE PLOT THICKENS

INDIAN FELT GOOD THAT he didn't have to kill Sam Phillips. Now all he had to do was to take care of Kent Eagle, get the herd to Dodge, sell the herd, collect the money for the herd, marry Serene, and get her back to Texas in time to pay off her bank loan.

After Sam Phillips rode off with his men, Indian went back into the saloon, found Wanda, and thanked her for her help with Phillips. He gave her two Double Eagle coins, and then he asked if she knew who Kent Eagle was.

"I know him. He's been hanging around the saloon for several weeks now. He usually comes in after eight o'clock and joins any poker game going on and wins most of the hands. Sometimes, it seems like he wins too many hands to be that lucky or that good."

"You know him all right. He's a pro with the cards. I guess he's a good player and lucky as well. Sometimes people think he's a little too good and too lucky. I know he's been in some shoot-outs with people who thought he was cheating, he's good at that too."

"Well, he's come close to a couple of shoot-outs here, but he talked the men out of it when he had a gun in his hand while they were still talking. He didn't have to shoot them. He just let them get up and leave."

"That's something new. In the past, he would have just killed them."

"Maybe he's concerned about getting crossways with Bat Masterson, our new Ford County sheriff who's vowed to clean up Dodge. They say he's a pretty tough hombre and has killed at least two dozen men.

"Just this year he captured 'Dirty Dave' Rudabaugh, a killer, rustler, and notorious gunfighter."

"Wanda, that sounds like a good reason for Eagle not to kill anybody in Dodge."

"Not many people have tried tangling with him since he took over as sheriff, and those that did have either been jailed or killed." "Thanks, Wanda, I think I'll just wait around to see if Eagle shows up tonight."

Indian went back to the table he had been sitting at earlier in the day and sat down to see if Kent Eagle would show up tonight.

Indian waited until around ten o'clock and finally told Wanda, "I guess Eagle isn't going to be coming in tonight."

She agreed but told Indian she'd heard Kent Eagle was staying over at the Dodge House, so he might check there.

Indian decided to take Wanda's advice and go over to the Dodge House to see if he was there.

Indian walked into the Dodge House and asked the man working at the front desk if his friend Kent Eagle was staying there.

The man said, "Mr. Eagle has been staying here for several weeks now, but this afternoon he checked out and said he was going back home in Texas."

Indian thanked him and went out to get his horse to ride back to the campsite where he had left Serene the night before.

After riding for about a mile or so out of Dodge, he could tell someone was following him, so he slowed his horse down and waited to see if the rider continued riding or if he would stop.

Indian drew his gun and waited; the rider kept coming, and a few more minutes passed, when he heard a voice say, "You leaving town, paleface?"

"Damn you, Robert. You were about to get shot coming up behind me like that."

"I wasn't worried. I knew you wouldn't shoot your old friend, would you?"

"Not if I knew it was you."

"From now on, be sure you know it's not me before you start shooting, OK?"

"OK, I think we better stop for the night and go back to the herd in the morning."

"I think that's a good idea. I'm getting pretty tired after looking out for you all day."

Indian and Robert stopped and unsaddled their horses, got their bedroll out, and lay down. Indian told Robert about what happened with Sam Phillips and about Kent Eagle leaving Dodge.

Robert could hardly believe it, but he was glad for Indian. Indian said, "Robert, I don't know what's going to happen, but

I still want you sticking close to me and watching my back." "No problem, my friend, good night."

*****

The following morning, Serene went down to the creek by herself to take a quick bath before it was time to fix breakfast and before it was time for Granny and her to get the cowboys up.

Granny wondered where Serene was when she woke up, and then remembered she had said last night she was going to go down to the stream to take a quick bath before everybody got up.

Serene found the water to be really cold; after all, it was December, so what did she expect it to be? She was soon out of the water and getting her clothes on when she thought she saw a couple of the cowboys watching her.

Serene said, "Hope you didn't get too much of an eyeful watching me dress."

The two cowboys said nothing, but suddenly they grabbed her, and one of them put a gag into her mouth. She tried to scream, but she could only make a little more than a whispering sound.

The two men tied her hands behind her back and carried her over to where three horses were waiting.

They lifted her up onto a horse and tied her feet to the stirrups; one of the men took a rope and put it through the horse's bridle while the other man mounted his horse and took the rope and tied it to his saddle horn.

Then the second man mounted his horse, and they rode away from the creek at a fast trot and headed in an easterly direction, riding toward the rising sun.

Serene couldn't figure out who these men were or where they were taking her. She only knew she was having a hard time staying in the saddle with her hands tied behind her back.

After some time, the men slowed their horses down, and one of them came back to her horse to check on her. He asked, "Do you need your hands tied in front of you so you can hold on to the saddle horn?"

Serene nodded she did.

The man took the ropes from her hands, and she took a swing at the man, who promptly slapped her in the face so hard it almost knocked her over to the side of her horse. The only thing that stopped her from falling off her horse was the rope tied around her foot to the stirrup.

Then the man tied her hands back up in front of her and told her she could hold onto the saddle horn to keep her from falling off her horse.

After that slap across her face, Serene knew these men weren't going to treat her nice if she put up a fight. She was going to have outsmart them rather than try to attack them. They were just too big and too strong for her.

The man said, "Miss Star, your life can be a lot easier if you just cooperate with us. We are going to be together for a long time, and the better you behave, the easier it'll be for all of us.

"We don't want to hurt you, but we can't let you go until our boss tells us to. He's a bad guy who would kill us if don't do what he says.

"We're going be to riding for a while, until we can flag down a train, then we're taking you on the train to Kansas City, where you will be staying with us until we get the word to let you go.

"You don't know it yet, but as of right now you have just become our sister. If you put up a fuss, we will have to restrain you and tell the people you're sick in the head, and we're taking you to see a doctor in Kansas City to see if he can help you.

"If you make a fuss when we get on the train, we'll tell the conductor you have crazy thoughts about being kidnapped, and what we're doing is trying to get our poor sister to Kansas City to see if the doctor can help her. 'She just keeps imaging all kinds of things, like she's a big ranch owner in Texas, and she has been on a cattle drive to Dodge with her cattle. Instead, she's been living in a sod house out here on the Kansas prairie with our parents.'

"One last thing: if you do try to escape, we'll have no choice but to kill you. Our boss wouldn't like it, but he said if all else fails, kill her.

"Do you understand everything about how it's going to be now?"

Serene nodded she understood.

The man said, "Miss Star, my name is Al, and my partner's name is Lightning. If you would like to get the gag out of your mouth, you'll have to promise you'll do your part and follow all the rules I just told you. Can you do that?"

Again Serene nodded she could.

Al untied Serene's feet and asked her to get off the horse so he could take her gag off.

For a moment, Serene thought about trying to give her horse a kick in the sides and take off, but she thought better of it. Her hands were still tied to the saddle horn, so she couldn't get off her horse either. What she did do was try to say she couldn't get off her horse because her hands were tied to the saddle horn.

Her trying to talk while she kept putting her head down toward the saddle made Al realize she couldn't get down because he had her hands tied to the saddle horn. He moved her foot out of the stirrup, put his foot in, rose up and untied her hands from the saddle horn. He then got back down to the ground and helped Serene get off her horse.

Serene stood there quietly as Al removed the gag from her mouth, and then she said, "Thank you, Al."

"You're welcome. Now you need to get back on your horse so we can get moving to try to be ready to board the train when it comes through."

Serene did as she was told. Al remounted his horse, and the three of them started riding east again.

They continued riding for four more hours without taking a break until they came upon the railroad tracks, and then Al said, "Let's stop here and rest the horses."

They stopped their horses, and the three of them got down from their horse. Serene was really sore from riding that long. She continued to move around to get some circulation going in her legs and butt.

For the first time, she really took a good look at the two men she was with. Al was about five foot seven with a ruddy face, blue eyes, dark-brown hair and maybe hundred and sixty pounds; Lightning was maybe five foot ten, with a beard, piercing green eyes, and hair the color of straw. He was as thin as a rail.

Both the men must have been in their early twenties; they were dressed in traditional cowboy clothes and hats, with bandanas around their necks.

Al carried one ordinary-looking six-gun, but Lightning had a pair of very gleaming six-guns with ivory handles, carried in a hand-tooled leather belt with matching holsters.

To Serene, those guns meant only one thing: Lightning was a paid gunfighter, and by the looks of the tools of his trade, he was a very successful one. She had heard about that kind of man all her life, but she had never known one or seen one before.

She thought about Indian's two guns and holsters and had to guess he would have been thought of as a gunfighter when he was a deputy sheriff in St. Louis, but he was a lawman. That was different, she guessed.

Al told Lightning to unsaddle two of the horses, take them out far away from the tracks, let them go, and then get back there before the train came through later in the afternoon.

Lightning unsaddled two of the horses, tied a rope onto their bridles, mounted his horse, and rode away with them.

Al told Serene she might as well rest while they waited for the train. She took one of the saddle blankets, laid it down, and used a saddle for a pillow—the way she saw her drovers sleep.

Maybe two hours passed before Lightning returned with his horse. After he arrived, he unsaddled his horse, let it loose, and then sat down on the ground next to Al to wait for the train.

Al told Serene, "When the train stops, I'm going to tell the conductor we were attacked by Indians and lost two horses. My brother and I were taking you to a doctor in Kansas City because you're just not right in the head and our ma and pa are really worried about you. Keep your mouth shut, and nobody will get hurt, including you."

Just as it was beginning to get dark, they heard the train coming. Al and Lightning took the saddle blankets and started waving them at the train. The train came to a stop when the engine was next to them.

The engineer asked, "What's the problem?"

Al answered, "We've been attacked by Indians, and they killed two of our horses. We're trying to get our sister to Kansas City to see a doctor who might be able to help her."

"What's wrong with her?"

"She's got something wrong in her head."

"What do you mean she's got something wrong in her head?" "She thinks everybody is trying to kill her or trying to kidnap her. She even thinks our ma and pa are trying to kill her. We heard there's a doctor in Kansas City that might be able to help her."

The train conductor came up just in time to hear what Al told the engineer about what was wrong with their sister. He said, "Come on aboard so we can get moving. We've got a schedule to keep. Hope you got money enough to pay for a train ride."

"Yes, sir, I think we do. How much is it from here to Kansas City?"

"That would be $60 for the three of you."

"Yes, sir, my pa gave me $100 to go there, so we've got the money."

Al reached into his pocket for the money, and the conductor said, "You can pay me when we're on the train."

"OK, sir. Is there someplace we can put our saddles and tack?" "Follow me, and you can stow your things in the baggage car."

"Yes, sir."

Al and Lightning picked up the three saddles, and Al said, "Sis, you bring along those bridles and blankets."

Serene said nothing; she just did as she was told.

When they got to the baggage car, a man inside the car opened the door, and they put their things inside.

When Serene handed the blankets up to baggage man, she didn't notice that her leather gloves, embroidered with yellow flowers, fell to the ground.

Then, the three of them followed the conductor back to one of the passenger cars, and they all got on it.

Once they were inside the train car, the train began to move, and the conductor said, "You can pay me now."

"Yes, sir." Al said.

Al took out three Double Eagle coins and paid the conductor for their train fare.

The conductor said, "Thank you. You three follow me. I'm going to take you back to another car. There's almost no one else in the car, so maybe your sister won't be so worried about being kidnapped or killed."

Al replied, "That's very kind of you, sir, thinking about my sister."

"Think nothing of it. I think it will be better for everyone. we don't want her bothering other passengers."

Serene kept her mouth shut and her eyes down, knowing Al had done a good job of planting the idea in the conductor's head that she was crazy.

The conductor said, "We'll be arriving in Kansas City late tomorrow afternoon, but we will be stopping in Hutchinson, where you can get something to eat at the Harvey House there.

Our train gets serviced there, and we change crews. I'll tell the new conductor who takes over for me about your sister."

When they stopped in Hutchinson, the three of them got off the train and had a good meal at the Harvey House; the next time they got off the train was in Topeka where they had breakfast. Then, late in the afternoon, they arrived in Kansas City.

After they got their saddles and tack, Al asked a man working at the station where they could find some place to stay near the station. He told him about a rooming house just a few blocks from the station.

Al told Lightning to stay with Serene and their things, and he would walk down to see if he could find some place for them to stay.

After Al left, Serene said, "Lightning, do you know how to talk? I've never heard you say anything."

In a soft Southern voice Lightning said, "Yes, ma'am, I know how to speak, but I don't have much to say."

"You certainly have a nice Southern drawl. Where are y'all from, anyway?"

"Are you making fun of me, ma'am?" "No, I just wondered where you're from."

"Nowadays, I'm not from anywhere. I used to be from Mobile, Alabama."

"I've heard that's a nice place. What are you doing out in the west?"

"Working, ma'am."

"They don't have any work in Alabama?" "No, ma'am, not my kind of work."

"I see."

Al came back with a man with a buggy to take them to the place he had found for them to stay. They loaded their saddles and tack into the back of the buggy, and the man drove them to the boarding house.

When they arrived at the boarding house, the man helped them bring their saddle and tack up to the third floor of the building, where they had three rooms in their apartment.

They had two bedrooms and a sitting room with a table and four chairs for a place to sit down and eat. The only door in or out of the apartment was in the sitting room.

Serene thought, "So this is to be my prison. It could be worse." The man told them they had a room down the hall with a bathtub, so she could take a bath sometime, she hoped.

After the man left them, Al said, "Serene, I'll get you some clothes and things tomorrow; you just make a list of the things you need to stay here for some time and I'll get them for you."

"Thank you, Al."

"You're welcome. Tell us which one of the bedrooms you want, and you can have it."

Serene went into each bedroom and selected the one that had some pretty wallpaper with pink flowers and green leaves.

She had a chamber pot—which was a good thing—a washbasin, and even a wall mirror.

Serene knew she had to make the best of this situation with whatever she could get, considering she was a prisoner and her life was in danger. She remembered the slap to her face; her face was still red.

She wondered what Indian would do after he found out she was gone. She knew he had to be going crazy, not knowing what happened to her. What about her cattle, and how was she going to be able to pay off her loan?

Serene decided she had to keep her wits about her and stay alive. Maybe she could play Al and Lightning against each other!

CHAPTER NINETEEN

WHAT DO WE DO NOW?

NDIAN AND ROBERT ARRIVED at the campsite to find people in turmoil. Indian shouted, "What in the hell is going on around here?"

Granny replied, "Serene's missing!" "What do you mean she's missing?"

"I mean she's gone, and we can't find her."

Indian got down from his horse, and everyone gathered around him. He asked, "With all of you people here, Serene just vanished?"

Granny replied, "Yeah, Indian, that's exactly what I mean." "Slow down, Granny, and tell me when you last saw her?" "Well, it was when we were going to bed last night. She told me she was going to get up early and go down to the creek to wash up before we started breakfast and get the drovers up."

"You didn't hear her when she got up this morning?" "Nope, I didn't see her or hear her."

"None of you cowboys saw or heard her this morning?" They all answered, "No, sir!"

"Alex, I want you and Miguel to get the men saddled up and get the herd moving toward Dodge. The buyer, Mr. Greenback, of the Chicago Cattle Company, is expecting them to be there in two days.

"We've got to finish the drive and get the cattle sold. Robert and I will see what we can do to find Serene. I wouldn't think she could have gone very far. At least I hope she couldn't.

"Granny, you get Charles Webster to help you with the wagon and the cooking. I'm sure he always wanted to be a cook on a trail drive.

Isn't that right, Charles?"

"Right, Boss! Whatever you say needs done, I'll do it." "Good! Robert, let's get started looking for the boss lady."

After saying that, Indian and Robert mounted their horses and rode down to the creek. They began riding up and down the creek, one on one side of the creek and one on the other side.

After about fifteen minutes, Robert said, "Indian, it looks like there are fresh tracks of three horses over here."

Indian rode across the creek and joined Robert where he was waiting for him.

Indian got down from his horse and said, "It looks like pretty fresh tracks all right. I think we better follow them to see where they take us."

Robert said, "What do you think it means to have fresh tracks of three horses leaving the creek?"

"I don't know what it means, but I do know it doesn't mean these riders were riding away from the campsite. So it's not any of our horses or men. I took a look around, and all of our men were at the campsite. So it wasn't any of our men who took her."

"I guess that's good."

"What I can't figure out is why someone would take her. Actually, that's a dumb thing to say. If you took one look at her, you'd know why any man would take her."

"You think so, dummy!"

"I told you it was a dumb thing to say." "You've got that right."

"Now I'm really worried. They might rape her, kill her, and then leave her body alongside the trail. Hell, they could leave her body anywhere out in this godforsaken country. Damn, I wish I could think of some other reasons for someone to take her.

"The pictures going through my mind right now are killing me thinking about what they might be doing to her.

"If they were Indians, they probably wouldn't kill her. They would make her one of their squaws."

"Indian, quit thinking about that and think about finding her quick."

"You're right, Robert. All my thinking about what men might be doing to her is clouding my judgment and not letting me think straight.

"One thing is for sure. If they wanted to kill her, they could have done it right there at the creek."

"That's good, Indian. So they didn't want to kill her. So why would they take her?"

"Robert, maybe to get at me, or maybe they're trying to keep her from getting back to Texas and paying off her loan. Somehow, I'll bet Kent Eagle is behind this.

"Hell, Robert, there could be a thousand reasons why they took a beautiful young woman like Serene, and none of them sound good to me."

Indian and Robert rode on for several miles, following the hoofprints when the prints were suddenly covered up so much with buffalo tracks that they didn't have any way of telling which way the riders went.

Indian said, "Robert, it looks like we're not going to be able to follow their tracks anymore. So far the only thing we seem to know is they were going in an easterly direction.

"I think I'll have to get back to the herd and make sure it gets to Dodge on time, get the cattle sold, and collect Serene's money so it's available to pay off her bank note.

"If you would, I would like for you to keep looking to see if you can either find them or pick up their trail again.

"After we get the cattle delivered to Dodge, I'll be staying at the Dodge House until I hear from you."

"Indian, you know I'll keep looking until I simply can't find any clues as to what happened to her."

"Thanks, Robert. I know you'll do everything you can to find her and bring her back to me."

"Indian, I'm going to keep riding east for a while to see if I can pick up their trail again. If I do, I'll follow it as long as I can until I find them. If I'm not back in Dodge in a week, it means I'm still on their trail. If I can't find anything, I'll send you a telegram to let you know where I'm at."

"Thanks, Robert, good hunting."

Indian turned his horse back toward where he left the herd and began the long lonely ride back to the herd, not knowing if he was doing the right thing or not.

The one thing he knew was he had to finish the job of getting the cattle drive completed, pay the men off, and get back to Texas before February first to get Serene's loan paid off so she didn't lose her ranch. And he had to find Serene!

Indian knew he had to take each of these tasks one at a time. Most importantly, he hoped Robert could find what had happened to Serene while he was taking care of all the other things.

After four hours, Indian caught up with the herd, and soon he made his way up to where Alex was riding point on the right side of the herd.

When Alex saw Indian ride up, he asked, "Did you have any luck finding Serene?"

"No. The only thing we found was fresh tracks of three horses leading away from the creek, and we followed them until the tracks were covered up by a herd of buffaloes passing through. Robert is trying to see if he can pick up their tracks again after the buffaloes passed by."

"Everybody is sure upset about Miss Serene and praying you'll find her and that she is OK."

"Thanks. I've been saying my prayers that she would be all right, that's for sure."

"I don't know who would want to hurt her. She's such a nice lady."

"Well, I'm not sure anybody is trying to hurt her. Maybe they just want her out of their way right now."

"I don't understand, Boss."

"Well, I can't talk about it right now because I need to go ahead and see how Granny's doing and find a place for our last campsite before we reach Dodge."

Indian urged his horse to break into a trot and begin pulling away from Alex.

Indian heard Alex shout, "OK, Boss. I'll see you later."

It didn't take long for Indian to see the chuck wagon, and he pushed his horse into a run; just before he got next to the wagon he slowed his horse down.

When he got beside the wagon, Granny saw him and shouted, "Did you find Serene?"

"No, we didn't. We did find tracks of three horses leading away from the creek, and we followed them until we lost track of them after a herd of buffaloes passed over their tracks. Robert is still searching to see if he can pick up the tracks again. I decided I'd better come back to be sure we got the herd to Dodge in the morning."

"Don't you think you should have stayed with Robert and kept hunting those tracks so you could find Serene?"

"Probably, but I know Serene would want me to be sure we got the herd into Dodge and get them sold so she has the money to pay off her note, so I came back to help get that job finished first."

"I guess you're right, Indian. She's sure worried about getting that note paid off."

"I know, Granny. How's Charles doing helping you cook?" "He's doing all right."

"Good! I'm going to go on to find the last campsite of the drive. See you after I find it."

Indian rode away, and suddenly he felt a very cold northwest wind blowing in his face. He didn't like it. They had made it on this long journey without any rain or snow, and he prayed it could wait one more day before they got snow or sleet or whatever was coming their way.

It didn't take long for Indian to find their campsite for the night since he had used the same one all year; the little creek still had a small amount of water running through it, and although there wasn't much of it, there was still a little bit of grass growing.

Indian turned his horse around, and both his horse and he liked it better with their backside to the wind. He kept thinking they had really been lucky not to have any bad weather on the trip. "Please God, just one more day of good weather."

When Indian got back to the wagon, he saw Granny and Charles were wrapped up in blankets, trying to keep warm and still be able to see well enough to keep the team going straight.

Indian said, "Granny, you don't have much farther to go before you get to the campsite; there's a big cottonwood tree next to a small stream, and you better be sure you've got everything tied down for the night because that wind is getting stronger every few minutes."

"OK, we'll try to get things tied down when we unload the wagon."

"Granny, I'm going to ride back to the herd to see how they are doing. See you when we get the herd to the campsite."

Indian continued riding to find the herd to make sure in this wind the herd hadn't veered off the trail.

Thirty minutes later he saw Alex and the herd slowly moving up the trail. Indian could see that neither Alex nor the cattle liked traveling with the raw bone-chilling wind blowing in their faces.

When Indian got up next to Alex, he said, "You only have maybe another hour to go before you get to the campsite."

"Good! I don't know how much longer the men can take riding into this cold wind. I can tell you that without having my rain slicker on, I'm about to freeze to death."

"Hang in there. We'll be there soon, and after we get the herd settled down for the night, we're going to need twice the number of men on night herd to be sure this wind doesn't spook the cattle into a stampede. We need to keep the cattle bunched up tonight to keep them from stampeding and straying."

"OK, Boss. We'll pack them up in a tight ball tonight." "Thanks, Alex. I'm going to ride back and talk to some of the other men and let them know what we're planning to do."

Indian rode back to talk to all the men so they knew they didn't have too much farther to ride. He also told them how he wanted to bunch up the cattle tonight.

By the time Indian had spoken to all the men, Alex and Miguel were turning the cattle to get them stopped for the night. It took over another hour and half to get the herd milling around and stopped for the night.

The wind hadn't slowed down any, and the temperature was continuing to fall. Indian could feel it in all his old, broken bones. The problem of getting older and living with several broken bones over the years was the cold weather always seemed to attack those bones.

Granny and Charles had a hard time trying to fix anything to eat for the men; they couldn't get a fire started because the wind kept blowing it out, and finally she said, "Guys, you're going to have to make do with whatever cold food we can find." Unfortunately, she couldn't find much for the men to eat.

Granny did find some hardtack in some tins and doled it out to the men.

Indian said, "Fellows, tomorrow night I'll make it up you. We'll have the best meal we can find in Dodge, and the only thing wrong is Serene will not be with us.

"After we get the cattle delivered to Dodge, I'll be spending my time finding Serene. I will find her, and when I do, I'll make the people who took her pay with their lives. You can bet on that."

Alex said, "We know you will, Boss, and if we can help, tell us what you want us to do."

"Thanks, Alex. I know you and your men would help in any way you could, and I appreciate it. But I know all of you have families to go home to, and as you know, my friend Robert is trying to pick up their trail. And the two of us should be enough to handle them."

The rest of the drovers shouted, "We'd help you, Boss!" "Thanks, men, but I have no way of knowing how long it will take to find Serene and bring her home. All of you have lives to get back home to. Serene has become my life, so she is all I have to live for."

Hearing that, all the men stood silently, and the only the sound they heard was the wind and the cattle in the background.

The next morning came earlier than normal. They couldn't have coffee or breakfast because the wind was worse than it was last night, so again, Granny couldn't build a fire.

Indian told the men, "Let's get the cattle moving and get them to Dodge before this storm gets worse."

Soon all the drovers were in their saddles and getting the cattle moving toward Dodge, the last five miles of the drive.

It was the worst miles of the drive with the wind blowing from the northwest at an ever-increasing speed, and after, what Indian guessed, they had gone a mile, the snow was coming down in snowflakes the size of silver dollars.

All the drovers had their rain slickers on and tied their neckerchiefs across their faces. The cords on their hats were straining to hold their hats down on their heads; and the hats often blew off and were saved only by the cord around their necks.

Indian wondered if they were even going to be able to make four more miles in this weather.

Indian was thankful they had the herd moving before it started snowing and that they had the four extra men helping the drovers in keeping the herd together and had Charles riding on the wagon with Granny.

Step by step, the herd and drovers continued to move closer to Dodge. Indian was now riding in front of the herd, guiding them to town.

They had been traveling for almost five hours without stopping, and the snow was now accumulating and drifting into some large snowbanks.

Indian could hardly see his horse's head, much less hundred feet in front of him, when he suddenly realized he was coming into Dodge. He continued to lead the herd toward the railroad's cattle pens, and when he reached the building with the office of Mr. Greenback, he leaned down from his horse and pounded on the office door.

Greenback came to the door and told him he didn't think he would be bringing the cattle in today. Indian said, "They're right behind me." Looking back to where Indian had come from,

Greenback could see the herd coming up to where his office was located.

Greenback told Indian to keep moving them down the street to their holding pens, and he would have his men there soon to count the cows as they came through the gates of the holding pens.

Indian nodded "OK" to Mr. Greenback and then spurred his horse on toward the holding pens.

Greenback's men came running out the office to open the gates of the pens and to get ready to count the number of Longhorns the drovers were driving into the pens.

In spite of the weather, they were able to get the cattle into the pens in just a little more than an hour.

When Greenback's men totaled up the number of Longhorns delivered to the pens, they had a total of 3,320 head.

Quickly, Indian totaled up the amount of money Serene was due for the 3,320 head of Longhorns at $35.75 each, for a total of $118,690.

By the time they got all the cattle in the pens, Mr. Greenback returned from the bank, and he gave Indian the $118,690 in cash.

As soon as Indian thanked Mr. Greenback, he told his men to come over to the Dodge House and he would pay them.

Indian rode over to the Dodge House, checked in, and went upstairs to his room. Only about ten minutes later, all the men who had been on the payroll arrived at his door.

Indian told them he would pay them one at a time; he said he would call each one of them into his room, and the rest would have to wait in the hallway.

Indian thanked each man individually for his help in getting the herd to Dodge and told them they should be damn proud of doing it. Each one of them appreciated hearing nice words from the boss.

Indian asked the men from Cuero, Texas, if they planned to go back home or if they were going somewhere else. All the men from the Cuero area said they were going home.

Indian told them that if they wanted to take the chuck wagon and the horses back to the Star Ranch he would pay each of them another $75 when they got back to Texas with the wagon and the horses. They all agreed to that.

He also told them that they would need to look after Granny Hayes to be sure she got home all right. They agreed to do that too.

After they agreed to look after Granny, Indian told them he would restock the chuck wagon with enough food to get them back to Cuero.

One last thing Indian told them as part of the agreement with the drovers was Alex would be in charge of the trip home, and if something happened to him, Miguel would take his place.

Indian paid the five men who had joined the drive late and who had warned him about Sam Phillips waiting in town to kill him and also told him that Kent Eagle was in Dodge too.

He thanked them for their help and gave them the bonus he had promised them for helping to get the cattle to Dodge. He asked them what they planned to do now, and they said they were going to try to go back home to Texas.

Indian told them they could ride along with his crew from Cuero who were taking the chuck wagon and the horses back to the Star Ranch if they wanted to, and they would be able to eat with them and not have to worry about buying food.

They said they appreciated it and would join the crew going to Cuero; they agreed that Alex would be in charge, and they would help with the horses. Charles said he would gladly help Granny with meals and driving the chuck wagon.

Indian made arrangement for a special dinner for all the hands at five thirty and also got rooms for all of them at the Dodge House.

The last person Indian spoke with was Granny Hayes, and Indian told her he didn't know what Serene had told her she would be paid for helping to cook on the drive. She told him she was to be paid $50 a month. Indian paid her $150 for the three months and also gave her the $100 bonus he paid the men from Cuero. She appreciated the extra bonus.

Granny said, "You know, Indian, I would have done it for nothing just to have the chance to do something useful, and I love Serene."

"So do I, Granny, and I'm going to bring her home."

Indian could see tears forming in Granny's eyes, and he felt a tear run down his own cheek.

"Don't you worry, Granny. I'll bring Serene home, all right? "Granny, all the men are going back to Texas to bring the chuck wagon and the spare horses home to the Star Ranch. I told them I would give each of the men from Cuero an additional $75 and buy the food for the trip home if they would do it. I would do the same thing for you if you're up to cooking some more for those useless cowboys."

"I'd be glad to do it. I wasn't sure how I was going to get back home. You said all the men are going to go to Texas, including the new men?"

"All of them, and Charles said he would be glad to help you cook and drive the wagon."

"Well, I don't know about how much he can help me cook, but he does what I tell him. That's more than most men would."

Indian had to smile at what Granny said and told her, "We need to get down to the dining room. It's getting pretty close to five thirty, and we don't want to be late for dinner. I don't know how you're going to make out, having a room all by yourself tonight."

Granny said, "Well, it will be different, but I'll make do somehow."

When Indian and Granny arrived at the dining room, they found all the men anxiously waiting for supper. They hadn't had much to eat since breakfast the day before yesterday, so they were hungry.

They were seated in a special room, away from the rest of the folks eating in the regular dining room, and couldn't stop talking about how hungry they all were.

When the servers began setting plates of food in front of them, suddenly a quiet fell over the room, and the only sounds heard were the sounds of knives and forks scraping plates.

Three courses later, talking resumed, just before coffee and dessert were served.

Most of the guests didn't know for sure if this was the best meal they had ever had, but it had certainly filled up some empty stomachs.

Indian waited for his guests to finish eating before he told everyone again what a great job they had done and wished them well. He said, "I'm looking forward to seeing all of you folks from Cuero when I get back to the Star Ranch, and to you other Texans, one big thank you for your help."

The last thing Indian said was, "May God be with you, wherever you go. And on behalf of Serene and myself, thanks to each of you one more time."

CHAPTER TWENTY

I'LL FOLLOW WHEREVER THE TRAIL LEADS

THE NEXT MORNING INDIAN looked outside and saw it had been snowing all night; the snow had drifted three to four feet high in some places on the street below.

Indian didn't know what he should do. He had a logistics problem; he needed to be in two places at the same time. First, he had to find Serene, but he had no idea of where she was. Second, somehow he had to get the money to the Cuero Bank & Trust to pay off the loan for Serene by February 1. At least he knew where the bank was since he saw it when he first rode into Cuero, Texas.

He hadn't heard anything from Robert yet, but it had only been a couple of days. So Robert probably hadn't got anywhere he could have sent him a telegram.

Indian decided that since he had told Robert he would wait a week at the Dodge House, he guessed he would have to do that just in case Robert couldn't pick up the tracks of the three horses again and came back to Dodge.

He went down for breakfast and saw most of his crew in the dining room having breakfast. He took a seat at a table with Alex and Granny. He asked how they slept, and both told him they almost couldn't get out of their beds this morning.

Granny said, "Indian, it was wonderful, but it sure makes me want to go home to my own bed."

"Granny, from the looks of the snow outside I'd say you might want to wait a day or two here in Dodge before starting back to Texas."

Alex said, "As much as I want to be home for Christmas, I don't want to risk everyone's life by starting out in this kind of weather."

Granny agreed with Alex.

Indian replied, "No, Alex, you're right. I don't want to see you start off in this weather, but you know what they say about Kansas weather, 'Wait a minute, the weather will change.' So by tomorrow, the weather may be just fine."

Granny said, "I hope so."

Miguel joined them and said, "Morning, everyone. It's starting to snow again. I sure wish I was back in South Texas."

Alex replied, "Don't we all."

Indian said, "I'm sure Serene wishes she had stayed in Texas." Granny replied, "No, Indian, she wanted to help bring the herd to Dodge and she can always be proud she did it. No, sir, as hard as it was for her, she's really glad she made the trip. She's a tough woman. I don't know who took her, but I know she'll be OK. She's got grit."

Indian said, "I guess you're right, Granny. I thought when I first met her she couldn't do all the things she did on this drive. What with being brought up in the east in some fancy school, I thought she'd want me to have her taken back to the ranch after the first couple of days, but I was wrong. You're right, Granny. She's got grit. She hung right in there no matter what I asked her to do." Alex said, "Boss, she's some woman to travel all the way from South Texas, help Granny cook meals, drive the horses pulling the wagon, and put up with all of us cowboys. I never heard her say one time anything was too hard for her to do."

Indian said, "No, Alex, she never complained about anything or anybody on all those miles we traveled. Serene was a real trooper. Now, I just have to find her and bring her home to Texas."

Later that morning, Indian put on all the warm clothes he could find to wear and ventured over to the train station. Even with everything he could find to wear to keep warm, by the time he walked to the train station, he was freezing.

He had a hard time getting the train station's door open due to the snowdrift that was up against the door; once inside, he walked to the telegraph office window and asked if there was a telegram for Indian Leader.

The clerk told Indian the lines were down somewhere between Dodge and Hutchinson; he said he was sure it was due to the heavy snow.

Indian thanked him for his time and told the clerk if he got a telegram for him, he was staying at the Dodge House.

Indian next stopped by the train clerk's counter and asked if there would be any trains through here today. The train clerk told Indian he didn't think so. They would have to plow the train's tracks before the trains could get through with the way the snow had drifted.

Indian thanked him and prepared to go back out into the cold to make his way back over to the Dodge House.

Indian kept thinking as he struggled to walk back in the snow to the Dodge House about how God had looked after them on the long drive from South Texas to Dodge. They didn't have any bad weather until the cattle were in the shipping pens in Dodge City. He thanked God again for bringing them safely to Dodge and asked God to help him find Serene and to keep her safe.

Two days later, the snow was gone and the weather had warmed back up and the trains were running again. Good news.

Granny, Alex, and Miguel told Indian over breakfast they were leaving this morning, heading back to Texas.

Indian told them he would go to the Dodge City General Mercantile Store to pay for the supplies after they had loaded all the supplies they needed for their trip back to Cuero.

Granny had prepared a list of items they needed for the trip and showed it to Indian. He checked over the list and told Granny, "It looks like you didn't miss anything," but he suggested they get some additional ammo to be sure they had enough in case they ran into any Indian trouble.

Granny told Indian she would be sure to get some extra ammo in case they needed it.

A little more than two hours later, the crew from Cuero left Dodge, and as they drove out of town, they saw their Longhorns being loaded onto cattle cars for their trip to the packing house in Chicago.

Indian saw the crew off and again thanked each of them for helping the Star Ranch deliver the herd of Longhorns to Dodge.

After the wagon and horses and men were out of sight, Indian walked over to the train station and went directly to the telegraph office. When Indian arrived at the window, the clerk said, "Mr. Leader, I was on my way to the Dodge House to bring you a telegram. I guess you saved me a trip."

The clerk handed him an envelope with a telegram inside. Indian ripped open the envelope and read what his telegram said

> Indian, I picked up the tracks of our three horses and followed them until they stopped at the train tracks. I flagged down the next train and talked with the conductor, who told me the train stopped for two men and a woman a few days ago in the same spot. He said they bought tickets to Kansas City. I'm sending this telegram from Hutchinson and plan to go on to Kansas City. I will send a telegram to you when I reach KC.
>
> Robert.

Indian was happy to get the telegram even if he wasn't sure what it meant about the two men who took Serene, and she went with them on the train to Kansas City.

Later that day, Indian heard a knock on his door; he got off the bed and opened the door. It was the telegraph clerk, who said, "I have another telegram for you, Mr. Leader."

Indian took the telegram and gave the clerk a sliver dollar for bringing the telegram to him.

The clerk thanked him, turned around, and headed back down the stairs.

Indian tore open the envelope and took the telegram out and read Indian, I'm in KC. I arrived yesterday and checked into the Kansas City Hotel. Talked to the people who sell train tickets, and they told me no one remembers selling tickets to a party of two men and a woman over the last few days. I plan to stay here to try to find where they've gone from here. You can reach me at the Kansas City Hotel, room 222.

Robert.

Indian sat down and wrote out a reply to Robert's telegram:

Robert, I plan to take the next train I can get to Kansas City. I will see you at the Kansas City Hotel soon. Indian.

Indian walked over to the train station and had the clerk send his telegram to Robert; then he went to purchase his train ticket. The railroad clerk told him the next train would be leaving in the morning at 4:00 a.m. Indian paid for his ticket and thanked him.

Indian sold his horse at the livery stable and took his saddle, bridle, and the rest of his tack over to the train station and asked if he could check these things to be picked up in Kansas City. He was told he could.

He walked back to the Dodge House, paid his bill for his room, and told them he would be leaving early tomorrow morning and going to Kansas City on the train.

On arriving in Kansas City, Indian picked up his gear from the baggage car and asked if they had a place where his things could be stored. He was directed to a storage room. Indian checked his gear and set out to find the Kansas City Hotel to meet Robert.

On arriving at the hotel, he asked directions to room 222 and was told it was up the stairs and down the hall to the left. He proceeded up the stairs and walked down the hall until he came to room 222. He knocked on the door, and Robert opened the door.

The two men went through their normal routine whenever they met. Robert said, "Hello, paleface, what kept you so long?"

Indian replied, "Hello to you, you old half-breed. I've just been hanging around waiting to hear something from you."

"I tell you one thing, if I hadn't found those three branded horses wandering around out there on the plains, I would never have figured out what happened to Serene. That led me to the idea they must have gotten on the train. So I started trying to find the train tracks, and when I did, I found where the train had stopped to take on passengers."

"OK, Robert, how did you figure out where the train stopped to pick up passengers?"

"I used an old Indian trick. I found Serene's leather gloves, you know, the ones with the yellow flowers on them."

"That's a helluva old Indian trick."

"Damn straight! So I sat down and waited for a train to come to the same spot that Serene must have gotten on the train when she lost her gloves."

"Damn, you're smart, Robert."

"I've been telling you that for years, but you never listen. "Anyway, when the train stopped, I let my horse loose and boarded the train and talked to the conductor who told me the train had stopped at the same place earlier in the week to pick up passengers.

I asked him about the passengers who boarded, and he told me it was two men and a young woman.

"The conductor said it was really pitiful about this beautiful young woman because her brothers told him they were taking her to a doctor in Kansas City to see if he could help her because he said she thinks everybody is trying to kill her. He said, 'Right now, she's even telling people we've kidnapped her.'

"Her brothers said her ma and pa didn't know what they were going to do with her.

"The conductor said he really hoped the doctor could help her." "Well, Dr. Robert, I hope you can help her by finding her. I think that's exactly the kind of help she needs.

"I haven't had much luck so far. In a town this size, it is not unusual to see two men and a woman on the street."

"Robert, I have to see if we can find out something about where Serene is pretty quick because if we can't find her soon, I'm going to have to go to Cuero to pay off her note at the bank by February 1 so she doesn't lose her ranch. I think that's why she's been kidnapped. They're trying to keep her from paying off her note so they can get her ranch.

"What were the brands on the horses you find out there on the prairie?"

"They had 'DE' on them."

"Just what I thought, Robert. They're working for a man named Kent Eagle. He has the ranch next to Serene's ranch. I knew him from St. Louis when I was a deputy sheriff in St. Louis. Only he went by the name Black Jack Eagle. He was a gambler and a killer. He killed several men in St. Louis, but he always had plenty of witnesses to say it was self-defense. So we could never hang him. "When I find him, he won't have enough witnesses left alive to lie for him. I'm going to kill them all."

"Careful, Indian, that might be a tall order. He might have a lot of men with him, and Serene probably wouldn't like it."

"Then those men had better stay out of my way, and I guess

Serene will have to forgive me after I kill them."

"Indian, I'll follow Serene's trail as long as it takes. We'll find her, and when we do, the men who took her will pay."

"Thank you, Robert. I'm going to have to leave in a couple of days if I have any chance of getting to Cuero, Texas, by February 1."

CHAPTER TWENTY-ONE

STOP FOR CHRISTMAS WITH THE FOLKS

TWO DAYS PASSED QUICKLY, and Indian and Robert didn't have any luck finding out anything new about the whereabouts of Serene. So Indian told Robert he had to leave; he didn't know how Robert could reach him until he got to Cuero.

Robert understood and assured Indian he would keep hunting for Serene.

Indian found he could take a train from Kansas City to Baxter Springs, Kansas, which would save him over a hundred miles of riding and several days of travel.

After he arrived in Baxter Springs, he went to the livery stable to buy a horse to make the trip to Cuero, and the owner told him he didn't have any horses for sale, but he told Indian a man who lived just south of town had several horses for sale.

Indian walked south out of town to find the horse ranch, and after walking for some time he saw a small sign that read, "Horses for Sale." Indian walked up toward a barn and small house and was soon met by several barking dogs, who accompanied him up to the barn.

Indian saw a man in the barn brushing a horse's mane, and the man turned to look at Indian. The man yelled at the dogs to shut up!

The dogs did as they were told, and the man said to Indian, "Cowboy, you look like you could use a horse."

"Yes, sir, I certainly need a horse, and I understand from the man at the livery stable you're the man to see."

"Yeah, I got lots of horses for sale. My name is Buddy Thompson."

Buddy put down his currycomb and walked up to Indian and put out his hand to shake hands.

Indian stuck his right hand out to shake Buddy's hand and said, "Buddy, my name is Indian Leader, and I need a horse that can take me all the way to South Texas and fast."

"Indian Leader, I've heard about you. You're the trail boss who's never lost a man on a drive."

Indian replied, "That's what I heard."

"Let me show you what I have. I'd be proud to have you riding one of my horses."

Buddy took Indian back behind the barn and gave a whistle and several good-looking horses came running up to the fence. Buddy said, "Anyone of these beauties can take you to moon if you're inclined to go there."

"Well, Buddy, if they could take me to the moon, I'd reckon they could take me to South Texas. How much are you asking for one of them?"

"Well, you know I get a little more money for my horses because when you buy a horse from Buddy you don't just get a horse, you get a Buddy horse. They're trained, not just broke."

"What do you mean they're trained?"

"Let me show you." He walked down the fence line and said, "All stay!" Then he said, "Prince, come here."

One of the horses left the other horses and walked directly to where Buddy was standing.

"What other kind of things can your horse do?"

"Let me show you. Prince, open the gate and come to me." Prince walked to the gate, pushed up the latch, and pushed the gate open with his nose.

Prince started walking to Buddy, and Buddy said, "Prince, close the gate."

Prince stopped and went back to the gate and pushed the gate closed.

Buddy said, "Lock the gate, Prince," and Prince pushed the latch down, locking it, and then came to Buddy.

"See what I mean, Indian? That's just some of the things my horses can do."

"OK, how much do you want for Prince?" "I want $200.00."

"Would you give me a little discount if I bought two of your horses?"

"Why would you want two horses?"

"Because I have a long way to ride, and I don't want to wear out a horse on the trip. If I had two horses, I could change horses and let one of them get some rest from carrying me."

"OK, I'll tell you what I'll do. I'll sell you two of my horses for $350.00 because I think you care about horses like I do."

"OK, it's a deal. Which one of the other horses gets along well with Prince?"

"All of my horses get along with any of them, but for the kind of riding you're planning to do, I think Captain would be the best one to go with Prince."

Then Buddy called out, "Captain, come here and don't forget to lock the gate."

Another one of the horses that had been standing at the fence went directly to the gate pushed up the latch, pushed the gate open, closed the gate back up, pushed the latch back down, and then came directly to where Buddy was standing.

Indian paid Buddy $350.00 and got a bill of sale for the two horses.

Indian looked over the two horses standing side by side and thought they looked like a matched team. They were both black in color, and both had four white stockings. Captain had a white blaze on his forehead, and Prince had a white star on his forehead. They were beautiful to look at, and Indian wondered how they would be to ride.

Buddy asked Indian if he needed a saddle to ride back into town to get his saddle and the rest of his gear.

Indian replied, "If you have a saddle I could use, it would be appreciated. So I can ride into town and get my gear. I guess I'm also going to need a bridle so I can lead the horse I'm not riding."

"I'll saddle Captain up for you, but you won't need another bridle because if you tell Captain or Prince to follow you, they will."

Indian said, "Are you sure one of them will just follow me if I tell them too?"

"I'm sure they will. Remember, they're Buddy horses, not your average old cow pony."

"All right, but if they don't, I'll be back through here someday, and I'm going to want my money back for the horse I lost."

"OK, if they don't follow you, you'll get your money back." Then Buddy said, "Prince, Captain come here."

Both horses came directly to Buddy, and when they did, Buddy said, "Indian, come stand next to me."

Indian stood by Buddy as he asked him to do. Then Buddy said, "Prince, Captain, this is Indian. He's your new boss, and you do what he tells you to."

Buddy turned to Indian and said, "Indian, put your hand to each one's noses."

Indian rubbed their noses.

Buddy said, "OK, Captain, Prince, Indian is your new boss. Do you understand?"

Both the horses looked at Indian and shook their head up and down.

Indian thought it was truly amazing; these horses acted as if they understood everything Buddy said to them.

Then Indian watched as Buddy saddled Captain and was amused at Buddy telling Captain what he was doing at each step of saddling him, beginning with putting on the saddle blanket and ending when he fastened the cinch.

All the while as Buddy was saddling Captain, he stood quietly with his ears up as he was listening to every word Buddy said.

Buddy said, "He's ready for you, Indian."

Indian took the reins from Buddy, put his foot in the stirrup, took hold of the saddle horn, slung his right leg over the saddle, and sat gently down on the saddle seat.

"You said you were headed south from here, didn't you, Indian? You can drop off my saddle and things on your way south."

"Thanks, Buddy. It shouldn't take me too long to return." Indian told Captain, "Let's go to town," and urged him to walk, and then Indian said, "Come on, Prince, follow me. Let's go to town."

Prince raised his head up and trailed right behind Captain. Indian found Captain was as smooth a ride as he had ever had on a horse, and no matter what pace Indian put Captain through, Prince stayed right with them.

On arriving back in town, Indian got his gear and saddled Prince while talking to him about each step Indian was doing as he saddled Prince, just as Buddy had done.

Prince reacted in the same way as Captain; he seemed to understand every word Indian said as he saddled him. Amazing!

Indian took the bridle off Captain, and when he did, Captain turned his head and looked back at the saddle, like "Hey, you forgot to take my saddle off."

Seeing this, Indian said, "It's OK, Captain, we'll get it off when we get back to Buddy's."

Indian thought, "My God, I don't know if it's a good thing when my horses act like they're smarter than me."

Indian mounted Prince and told Captain to follow, and Indian rode out of Baxter Springs, Kansas, on Prince, while Captain followed right along with him.

When they arrived back at Buddy's ranch, Indian saw Buddy waiting for him, and Buddy asked, "How do my horses ride?"

"Buddy, it's like gliding on a rocking chair, smoothest ride I've ever had on a horse."

Hearing that, Buddy beamed from ear to ear.

Buddy unsaddled Captain, and Indian and his horses were off to Texas.

As soon as Indian left Buddy's ranch, he entered Indian Territory since Buddy's ranch sat right on the line dividing Kansas and Indian Territory.

Indian planned to make at least fifty to sixty miles every day to be sure he got to Cuero in plenty of time to pay off the note for Serene.

It was now December 20, and as soon as Indian rode into Indian Territory he thought about his folks and Christmas. He thought he should get something for them for Christmas and should stop to see them on his way to Cuero.

Before he went any farther, he turned Prince around and rode back into Baxter Springs and rode directly to the general store he had seen there earlier.

He stopped Prince in front of the store, and Captain came up alongside Prince. Indian said to his horses, "Stay."

Indian got off Prince and went inside of the general store and wondered what he could get for his mother and father for Christmas.

Indian looked around the store and saw a case full of jewelry, and in it, Indian saw a beautiful pin with three pearls mounted on a gold leaf-shaped pin.

He asked the storekeeper the price of the pin and was told it was forty dollars. Indian said he would take it as a Christmas present for his mother.

Indian continued to look at the items in the case and saw a gold wedding band; he asked about the price of it and was told it was forty dollars. Indian said he would take that too.

Then he had to think of something he could buy for his father. In the same case, he saw a lovely gold pocket watch with a chain. The clerk said it was seventy-five dollars.

Indian hesitated for a moment and the clerk said, "If you buy the ring, pin, and watch, you can have all of them for $140."

Indian said, "OK, I'll take all of them."

Indian went back to where his horses were waiting for him and noticed a couple of men who had been inside the general store seemed to be checking him out when he was buying the Christmas presents for his loved ones.

Indian mounted Prince and rode out of Baxter Springs toward Indian Territory. He soon noticed the two men were either following him or simply going in the same direction he was.

Indian decided to find out which it was: following him or just going his way.

Indian brought Prince into a run, and the two men did the same. Indian then knew the two men were following him.

Indian continued to keep Prince running, with Captain staying right next to him. Not long after Indian crossed into Indian Territory, he saw a big cottonwood tree next to Spring River and rode directly to it and got off Prince. Captain stopped next to Prince and Indian told them to stay.

Indian pulled his rifle out of the scabbard attached to his saddle; he moved away from his horses and turned to face the men following him. He got behind the cottonwood tree and dropped down to the ground.

The men saw that Indian had stopped, and they began firing at him with their pistols. Then Indian fired his rifle once, and one man fell from his horse; he fired a second shot, and the second man fell to the ground.

Indian saw both men moving around on the ground. Indian got on Prince, and with Captain following behind them, he rode back to where the men had fallen. But by the time he got to them, they were both dead.

Indian decided that when they saw him buying Christmas presents, they thought he had money, and they were going to take it. They had no idea of how much money he was carrying with him to pay off the note for Serene. Now, they had no use for money.

Indian unsaddled their horses and turned them loose; he checked the men's bodies over to see if they had any ID, but he found nothing to tell him who they were.

Since he didn't have any way to bury them, he left their bodies where they lay.

Indian took their guns and holsters with him since they were not going to be of any use to them anymore, and he didn't want to just leave them lying out here.

Indian followed the Spring River until it joined the Neosho River; then he continued to follow it until he came near the Cherokee Indian Reservation. Then he rode east to get to where his folks lived.

Early in the afternoon of December 24, Indian arrived at his folks' small wooden home located on a small piece of land inside the reservation.

When he rode up to the house, a small brown-and-white dog greeted him, wagging its tail. His dad always had to have a dog around, though his mother said it was just having another mouth to feed since they were never good for anything else.

Indian had heard her say that for as long as he could remember, but the dogs his father had were either on his mother's lap or curled up on the floor beside her feet.

His mother was working in the kitchen when he rode up, and she saw him through the little window by her kitchen cabinet work area. She screamed, "Indian, you're home."

She ran out of the cabin door and waited for him to get off his horse.

Once he was on the ground, she put her arms around his waist and held him as tight as she could and said, "I thought you were never going to come home to see us again."

Indian picked her up and held her in his arms as he told her he loved her and then said, "Ma, don't say that. You know I come as often as I can and still do my job."

"I know, Son, but seeing you every day wouldn't be often enough for me."

"I'm sorry, Mom. I'll try to do better. Where's Pa? I have something to tell both of you."

"He went to the trading post to buy some things for our Christmas dinner. He should be back soon."

Indian's mother, like every mother in the world asked, "Son, would you like to have something to eat?"

"Sure, Mom. What do you have that's not too much trouble for you?"

"How about a couple of eggs and some slices of bacon?" "Thanks, sounds great, Mom."

"Sit down and tell me what you've been doing while I fix your eggs and bacon for you."

"Mom, I'm on my way back from Dodge City where we just delivered three thousand head of cattle we brought there from a ranch near a little town called Cuero, Texas. It's way down in the south part of Texas. Right now, I'm going back to Cuero to pay a bank loan for a woman named Serene Star."

"Son, that's a really pretty name."

"Yeah, Ma, she's as pretty as her name." "How come you're doing that for her?" "It's kind of a long story."

"I've time to listen to you, Son."

"I would like to wait till Pa comes home from the trading post so I don't have to tell the same thing twice."

"OK, I can wait. I'm always waiting for you or your pa." "Thanks, Ma. I want to tell you the whole story."

Indian's mother put his plate of eggs and bacon on the table with a loaf of fresh-baked bread along with some butter and apple butter.

Indian sat down at the table and savored every bite of the food his mother sat before him.

After he finished his meal, his mother said, "I think I hear your father coming now."

Charlie Whitebird came inside the house and asked, "Moonlight, who do those horses belong to out by the barn?" Then he saw Indian rushing up to him and said, "Oh, Son, I'm so glad to see you. It's been too long."

Indian put his arms around his father and said, "I'm so glad to see you, too, Pa. I love you so much."

His father said, "God, I've missed you. Tell me how you're doing. How long can you stay, Son?"

"I'm fine Pa. I can't stay long, but I will stay home to be with you and Mom for part of Christmas Day."

"That's wonderful! So what have you been doing?"

Indian began to tell his folks about his latest cattle drive. "I've just finished the hardest cattle drive I've ever had. I was going to Cuero, Texas, to drive three thousand head of Longhorns for a man named Ben Star. I rode into a little town in Texas to get something to eat, and a fellow came out of a saloon and said he was going to kill me. So I had to kill him. I found out later he was a young man named John Phillips. After I left town, two of his brothers followed me, and I had to kill them to stay alive.

"When I arrived at the Star Ranch, I found Ben Star had been killed by rustlers, and his daughter, Serene Star, was now the owner of the ranch.

"She told me they had lost two herds sent on trail drives early in the year and she was desperate to get her cattle to market. It seems her father had taken out a loan on the ranch at the Cuero Bank to buy additional land to add to his ranch, and it was due to be paid on February first.

"She said she didn't have enough money to pay off the mortgage without getting her cattle sold.

"She told me the bank said if she couldn't pay off the loan, they intended to foreclose on her ranch. She couldn't let that happen since her father spent fifty years building the ranch to leave for her. "I never wanted to do a trail drive this late in the year, but I couldn't let her down. So I agreed to do it.

"So, I put together a crew from the local area because most of her cowboys quit after her father was killed because they wouldn't work for a woman and they were also afraid they would be killed by these rustlers.

"Because Serene's cook also quit, she and a woman friend of hers, called Granny Hayes, accompanied us on the trail drive as our cooks. They did a great job cooking and looking after the drovers and me.

"I was attacked two more times on the drive: once by a bartender who thought he could earn the reward the Phillips brothers offered to anyone who would kill me, and then I had to kill two more of the Phillips brothers.

"I said they did a great job of looking after me because the bartender shot me in the side, and they nursed me back to health."

Mom asked, "Indian, how bad were you hurt?"

"Not too bad, Ma. After getting patched up and a good night's sleep, I was able to do my job the next morning."

Pa said, "I'm glad, Son. Did you make it all right with the cattle to where were you going?"

"Pa, we were going to Dodge City, and yes, we made it there just in time to put the cattle in the shipping pens before we had a blizzard."

Ma said, "Son, it sounds like this was an awful trip."

"Well, it got worse. Someone kidnapped Serene the day before we got to Dodge, and we haven't been able to find her. Then, just before we got to Dodge, I found out another one of John Phillips's seven brothers had brought along some gunmen to kill me after I had killed five of his brothers. He was waiting for me in Dodge."

Pa said, "Since you're here, I guess you had to kill them, too."

"No, I was lucky enough to talk to Sam Phillips. I told him it was time to quit trying to kill me because I was sure getting tired of killing the Phillips. He also knew I could have killed him instead of talking to him, so he agreed to quit trying to kill me or have me killed. He also agreed to quit offering a reward for killing me, which was really good."

Ma asked, "So why are you going to Cuero, Texas, if this Serene Star was kidnapped?"

"I've got to get there and pay off her loan. Then I've got to find her because I love her, and we're going to get married!"

Ma said, "Oh, Son! That's wonderful, but what if you can't find her?"

"That's not an option. I've got to find her. I won't stop looking for her until I do. You know my friend, Robert Smiley? He's helping me find Serene. The morning Serene was taken, Robert and I followed the tracks of three horses until we lost their tracks due to a herd of buffaloes passing over them.

"Because I had to get back to finish getting the cattle to Dodge, I had Robert keep looking, and he found the three horses and discovered three people had flagged down a train. Robert did the same and found out two men had taken her to Kansas City, and the best we can find out, we believe, she is still being held there."

Pa asked, "How did Robert Smiley come to be with you? His folks told me he went to Colorado to look for gold."

"I met him in the trading post on the Red River in the southwest part of the Territory. He was on his way home after not finding any gold. I hired him to help keep me alive."

Pa said, "Well, he's big enough to scare most people off. You two were always getting into trouble."

"Now, Pa, you know we weren't always in trouble."

"No, you two were angels compared to the kids on this reservation nowadays. Kids now are brats. They got no respect for nobody."

Pa asked, "Indian, where did you get those two beautiful horses I saw out by the barn?"

"I bought them just across the border on a ranch near Baxter Springs, Kansas. Those horses aren't just beautiful, they have been trained to do things I never knew a horse could do.

"Pa, it's unbelievable what they can do. I wish I had time to show you, but I've got to go on to Cuero tomorrow."

Ma said, "Indian, you can't go tomorrow. It's Christmas."

"I know, Ma, but I've got to get to Cuero before February 1." Pa said, "Son, if you leave tomorrow, you'll break your mother's heart."

"You're right, Pa. I'll stay for Christmas since it's been so long since I was home on Christmas."

Ma said, "Good. That's settled."

Christmas came and Indian woke up and could smell his mom cooking bacon. He got up, washed up, and dressed; then he looked in his saddlebag and took out the presents he had bought for his folks.

He went into the kitchen and saw his mother standing by the stove cooking; she turned around and said in a cheerful voice, "Merry Christmas, Indian."

"Merry Christmas, Mom. Your bacon sure smells good."

"I hope it is good. We need a nice breakfast before we go to church."

Indian took the pin he had bought for his mother and handed it to her and said, "Merry Christmas, my dear mother."

His mother took the pin from Indian and looked it over with a gleam in her eyes and said, "Indian, it's beautiful. Thank you so much. I'll wear it every day."

Just then Indian's father came in and said, "Merry Christmas, Son."

Mom said, "Look what Indian gave me," as she was putting the pin on her dress.

"It's really beautiful, Ma."

Indian said, "I've got a Christmas present for you too, Father," and he handed the gold pocket watch with the gold chain to his father.

Dad said, "Indian, it's really beautiful. I've never seen a watch as beautiful as this one. Thank you so much."

Before Indian could tell him he was welcome, his mother left the room and came back with the finest-looking buckskin outfit Indian had ever seen. It was the finest outfit his mother had ever made for him; it had a leather fringe across the top of his shirt above the two pockets, and leather fringe sewn all the way down the seams of his pants.

Along with the fringe on his shirt, his mother had placed small silvery beads along the fringe.

Indian said, "Mom, it's so beautiful! Thank you so much! You know I love wearing the clothes you make me. I have to go change right now."

Mom said, "OK, Indian. Go change, and by the time you come back, our breakfast will be ready."

Indian soon returned wearing his new buckskin clothes, just as his mother was setting breakfast on the table. parents had a chance to show off the Christmas presents Indian had given them to their friends. They were so happy with the gifts Indian brought them and told everyone what a wonderful son he was.

After they returned from celebrating Christmas at church, his mom started working on their Christmas dinner, which she planned to have later in the afternoon.

Indian and his father spent time talking about what Indian should do in the future. They both knew trail drives would soon be ending, and there would be no need for trail bosses since the railroads were laying tracks every day closer and closer to Texas.

Indian said, "Well, if I can find Serene, and she's still inclined to marry me, I guess I'll help her run her ranch."

"What if you don't find her?"

"I guess I'd go back to being a lawman, but, Pa, I'm going to find her. You can count on that."

"Indian, I don't think you have to worry about jobs for lawmen going away anytime in the future."

"Reckon not, Pa."

Indian's mother came and joined them, and they spent the rest of the day talking about what was going on at the reservation and about the people Indian knew who lived there.

After a late Christmas dinner, Indian said, "I'm sorry, but I have to leave tonight and ride some of the miles I need to get to Cuero by February 1."

Before he left, Indian changed out of his buckskins back into work clothes and again told his mother how much he loved his new clothes.

Indian held each of his parents and kissed them good-bye and told them he loved them.

He mounted Captain and told Prince, "Follow me," and he slowly rode away from his folks' home.

Indian shouted back to his folks, "Merry Christmas," as they continued to watch him until he was out of sight.

CHAPTER TWENTY-TWO

ARRIVING IN CUERO, TEXAS

INDIAN ARRIVED IN CUERO, Texas, on January 29, and rode directly out to the Star Ranch to see how the men were getting along. When he arrived at the ranch, he found Lloyd Johnson talking to the other ranch hands and telling them what they needed to do for the day.

When Lloyd saw Indian he said, "Mr. Leader, you're back. Where is Miss Serene and the rest of the men?"

Indian stepped down from Prince as Captain stood alongside them.

Indian said, Lloyd, it's good to see you and the rest of the men. I've got a lot to tell you but first I need a cup of coffee and a bite to eat."

Lloyd replied, "Sure, Mr. Leader. Come on into the kitchen, and we can get you some coffee and something to eat."

Indian followed Lloyd inside the kitchen and found a man that he didn't know working there.

Lloyd asked the man to bring Mr. Leader a cup of coffee and asked him to fry up some eggs and stuff for him.

The man brought the coffee and asked, "Mr. Leader, what would you like for breakfast?"

Indian replied, "About four eggs and some bacon. If you have some that would really help."

The man answered, "Coming right up."

The man turned around and went to the stove to cook breakfast for Indian.

After Indian had three more cups of coffee and had eaten every scrap of food from his plate, he said, Lloyd, we got the cattle to Dodge on time, but the day before we got to Dodge, someone kidnapped Miss Star.

"So far, we haven't been able to find her, but a friend of mine is still trying to locate her. We tracked her and her kidnappers to Kansas City but haven't been able to find her yet.

"I came back to take care of some business for her because it's something that has to been done in Cuero."

Lloyd said, "You mean to pay off the bank note before February 1?"

"Yes, Lloyd. That's exactly what I mean."

"I know about the note because a few days ago a fellow from the bank and Kent Eagle came over to look around the ranch, and Eagle said, 'I'm buying the ranch in a few days,' and he asked me if I would stay on to work for him.

"I didn't give him an answer, but I wouldn't work for him even if I had to leave Texas to find a job."

"Lloyd, I don't think you will have to leave Texas to find a job because he's not getting this ranch."

"Good, I hate that son of a bitch because I'm sure he's the one who either killed or had Mr. Star killed."

"I'm pretty sure you're right, Lloyd, but it's hard to prove."

"What can I do to help you, Mr. Leader?"

"For one thing, you can stop calling me Mr. Leader. Just call me Indian. OK, Lloyd?"

"Sure, Mister, sorry, Indian. You tell what else I can do to help you."

"Lloyd, I'm going to go over to the bunkhouse and take a little nap. Then I'm going to wash up and change my clothes, and then I'm going to town to take care of some business for Serene."

After Indian had a couple of hours' sleep, he got up, washed, dressed in the new buckskin outfit his mother had made for him for Christmas, and strapped on both of his guns. He asked Lloyd to have one of the men bring him a fresh horse to ride to town.

Lloyd had one of the men bring Indian a horse with Indian's saddle and gear on it so he was ready to go to town.

Indian thanked the man who brought his horse, mounted, and rode off toward town.

When Indian arrived in Cuero, he rode directly to the Cuero Bank & Trust and tied his horse in front of the bank.

Indian walked into the bank, and everyone looked up at him and wondered who the stranger was and if he was planning on robbing the bank.

Indian told a clerk he wanted to speak to the bank manager. He was directed into a small office on one side of the bank.

When Indian entered the office, the man who had been working behind the desk rose and said, "I'm Bradford Wilson, president of the bank. How can I help you?"

Indian replied, "I'm here of behalf of Miss Serene Star, and I wish to pay off the bank loan her father took out." "Where is Miss Serene?"

"I'm sorry to say that she was delayed returning home at this time, so I'm here to pay off the loan for her."

"What did you say your name was?"

"I didn't say my name, but it's Indian Leader."

"Well, I'm sorry, Mr. Leader, but I'm afraid you can't do that. Only Miss Star can pay off the loan."

"Mr. Wilson, you will have to show me the law that says I can't pay off the loan for her."

"Well, it's not a law. It's bank policy."

Indian took out his pistol and pointed it directly at Mr. Wilson and said, "Mr. Wilson, I think you better look again. I believe that policy has just been amended."

Mr. Wilson looked at Indian and the gun he was holding and said, "I'm really sorry, Mr. Leader, but I no longer make policy at the bank. Mr. Kent Eagle now owns the bank."

Indian cocked the hammer on his gun and said, "I'm counting to six, and if you don't get out the note the Star Ranch owes the bank, I'm going to start by shooting your right ear off. Bullet two will be to take your left ear off, number three will be in your left arm, number four will be in your left leg, number five will be in your right leg, and number six will be right between your lovely blue eyes.

"Let's see if you understand what I've just told you, Mr. Wilson. Nod your head if you understand."

Mr. Wilson nodded his head to indicate he understood.

Indian said, "You tell Mr. Eagle if he doesn't like having the Star note paid off, I'll be glad to meet with him and discuss it.

In fact, I'll been waiting over at the saloon till seven o'clock tonight in case he wants to talk with me."

Mr. Wilson asked, "Is it all right if I open the drawer on my desk to get the loan paper and note out for the Star Ranch loan?"

"It will be OK, but what you pull out of the drawer better be paper or you're dead, got it?"

Mr. Wilson slowly opened the desk drawer and pulled out a file folder; he opened the folder and took out the Star Ranch note and loan paper and showed them to Indian.

Indian said, "How much is the loan balance?"

"Its $35,000, plus $2,100 interest, a total of $37,100."

Indian put his gun back in its holster, opened his saddlebag, and took out a bank bag from the Bank of Dodge City. He opened the bank bag and counted out $37,100 and handed it over to Wilson. He said, "Mark the note 'paid in full' and get me a receipt for the money, and you and your teller both sign the receipt."

Wilson did as he was told. He marked the note "Paid in full" and signed a release of the lien on the Star Ranch and signed a receipt and had a teller sign the receipt as well.

Wilson said, "I'll see Mr. Eagle gets your invitation to meet him at the saloon before seven o'clock tonight."

Indian said, "Mr. Wilson, I see you're a reasonable man, and if you're able to get Mr. Eagle out of the bank business, I believe Miss Star will continue to do her banking business with you."

Indian stuck his hand out, and Mr. Wilson shook it.

Indian took the receipt, the note, and the loan papers and put them in his saddlebags. He took them over to the saloon and asked the bartender to put his bags somewhere safe and told the bartender if anything happened to him, he was to make sure that Serene Star got them.

The bartender told him he would lock the bags up, and if something happened to him he would see that Miss Star got the saddlebags.

After Indian left the bank, Mr. Wilson got his horse and rode to the Double Eagle Ranch to tell Kent Eagle that a man had come into the bank and forced him to take the money to pay off the note on the Star Ranch.

Kent Eagle was not happy to be told Wilson had let someone pay off the note on the Star Ranch since he was ready to take over the ranch on February 2; he had big plans for it.

Wilson said, "I didn't have a choice. He had a gun pointed at me the whole time he was paying off the note. The man said to tell you if you didn't like it, he would be waiting at the Cuero Saloon until seven o'clock this evening to discuss it with you."

"That's what he said, did he? Well, I'm certainly planning on it, as he said, to discuss it with him. What did the guy look like?"

"I don't know. He was just a tall guy about your height. Oh, you know, he just looked like another cowboy, but he did tell me his name. It was something like Leader or Lincoln."

"OK, you ride back to town and go back to the bank while I make plans to take care of this cowboy."

Mr. Wilson mounted this horse and rode back into town. When he arrived back in town, Mr. Wilson returned to the bank.

Kent Eagle had hired a new gunslinger by the name of Texas Tom. He told him he wanted him to kill a man waiting for him at the saloon in Cuero but told him to stop at the telegraph office first to send a message for him to Al Beckett.

His message to Al read Al, no longer want the package you have been holding for me. Get rid of it, never want to see it again. KE

After Texas Tom finished sending the telegram, he rode directly to the saloon and tied his horse in front of it. He walked into the saloon and went straight up to the bar and told the bartender he wanted a whiskey.

The bartender poured him a drink and asked if there was anything else. Texas Tom told him, "No, just leave the bottle."

After Texas Tom finished his drink, he turned around to see who this man was who said he would be waiting for Mr. Eagle.

When he saw Indian sitting at a table in the back of the saloon, he looked him over carefully and realized he had seen this man before but couldn't remember where he had seen him.

Then Texas Tom saw the two guns resting in the hand-tooled leather holsters and the way the holster on his left side was angled. He knew he had to be that fast-drawing deputy from St. Louis he had heard about over the years.

Indian sat very still, waiting to see what this man was going to do; he wondered if Eagle had sent him instead of coming to meet him.

Indian dismissed the idea quickly because he knew Kent Eagle thought he could take care of himself and didn't need anyone else.

Texas Tom continued to stand at the bar and just looked at Indian. Then he said, "I understand you wanted to talk with Mr. Eagle about something, and he asked me to take care of it for him." Indian replied, "My messenger may not have delivered my message to Mr. Eagle very clearly. I said I wanted to talk with Mr. Eagle, not some cheap flunky, so where is he?"

"Mr. Eagle said if you had anything you wanted to talk to him about, you could take it up with me."

"What makes you think I would bother talking with you? You're just some overpaid cowboy that doesn't know which end of a horse you're supposed to get on. I guess you're one of the bunches who have been rustling cattle, stealing two herds of Star cattle while they were on their way to market, then kidnapped Serene Star, and killed her father!"

"Mister, you're making a lot of accusations about things you don't have one ounce of proof that I've done any of those things, do you?"

Hearing this conversation, the bartender moved out from behind the bar and went out the back door of the saloon.

The cowboy continued to stand right where he had been standing as Indian watched his every move.

After Indian found the man wasn't going to say anything more, Indian asked, "Did you come here just to talk for your boss, or did you plan on doing something else?"

Indian then said, "Friend, if you want to walk out of this saloon alive, I'll tell you how you can do it. All you have to do is tell me where Eagle is holding Serene Star. Then you can walk out that door, get on your horse, ride out of town, and never come back. Got that?"

"Mister, I'm telling you I don't know anything about where Serene Star is, and I've never had anything to do with stealing cattle from the Star Ranch."

The saloon doors swung open, and three cowboys came into the saloon and started toward the bar. Indian said, "You fellows better stand back away from the bar if you don't want to be standing next to a liar, cattle rustler, murderer, and kidnapper!"

The three men stopped in their tracks just in time to see Texas Tom draw his gun, but before he could aim it, Indian fired two shots, hitting him twice, once in the stomach and once in his chest; then he fell to the floor.

Indian got up from his chair and walked over to where the man lay. He picked up his gun, laid it on the bar, and turned him over to see if he was still alive.

The man was still breathing and said, "Too bad, cowboy, you're too late. I sent a telegram for Eagle just before I came here, telling the men holding Serene to kill her."

Texas Tom choked twice and then died.

The doors of the saloon burst open, and the sheriff and the bartender came in. The sheriff asked, "What's going on in here?"

Then he saw the man lying dead on the floor and Indian standing over him with his gun in his hand.

The sheriff said, "Put the gun on the bar, cowboy."

Indian did as the sheriff told him; he laid his gun on the bar and turned around to face the sheriff.

When the sheriff saw Indian still had another gun in his holster, on his right hip, he said, "Cowboy, take that other gun out of its holster with your left hand and lay it on the bar next to your other gun."

Indian again did as the sheriff told him. With his left hand, he took the gun out of its holster and laid it on the bar next to his other gun.

Then the sheriff asked, "What's your name, cowboy?" "Indian Leader is my name."

"What are you doing here in Cuero?"

"I just finished a trail drive for the Star Ranch, and I came here to pay off a bank note for Serene Star."

"Why didn't she come and pay off her own loan?"

"Sheriff, that's a good question, but the answer is she couldn't." "Why not, cowboy?"

"Because she's been kidnapped by men who are working for Kent Eagle, just like the man lying on the floor was working for Eagle. He was sent here to kill me."

One of the cowboys who came into the saloon with his two friends said, "Sheriff, the man lying on the floor said just before he died that he had sent a telegram for Mr. Eagle to kill Serene Star just before he came in here."

The other two cowboys said, "That's right, Sheriff, we all heard him, and he drew first before this man shot him."

The sheriff asked Indian, "Are you a professional gunfighter? If you're not, how come you have a holster made up special for the left side of your body for a second gun?"

"Sheriff, I used to be a deputy sheriff for St. Louis County, Missouri. I found with this design I could draw my gun easier if I was sitting on my horse or sitting down. It saved my life a few times when I was a deputy.

"Sheriff, I knew Kent Eagle when I was a deputy in St. Louis, only he went by the name Black Jack Eagle. In fact, he was involved in several shootings when he was gambling.

"We knew he killed these men, but he always had plenty of witnesses who said the other man drew first. We knew he was a killer but couldn't ever prove it.

"I've been a trail boss for cattle drives for several years now, and I took a herd for Star Ranch to Dodge.

"The day before we got to Dodge City, two men kidnapped Serene Star. We were able to track them to Kansas City, but we haven't been able to find her.

"I made the trip to Cuero to pay off a note for Miss Star before February 1, because the bank had threatened to foreclose on her ranch if she didn't get the loan paid on time."

The sheriff said, "I don't know what's going on, but the Cuero Bank has always worked closely with all the ranchers till recently. Suddenly, they threaten to foreclose on every rancher around here, but I don't know why."

"Mr. Wilson told me Kent Eagle owns the bank now."

"That probably explains it. He's trying to get control of every ranch in the county for some reason or the other."

"Sheriff, maybe he found out the railroad was coming this way, and he wanted to sell property to them and make a lot of money."

"Thanks, Indian. You can go whenever you want to. I'll get the undertaker to take care of this man's body. After looking at this man's face, I know who he is. It's Texas Tom. I've seen his picture on so many posters because he was wanted dead or alive. There's even a reward for him, so I guess we're going to owe you some reward money. Well, I know a good place for him now, out there on boot hill."

Indian asked the bartender to get his saddlebags for him and told the three cowboys, "I want to buy each one of you a bottle as thanks for your help."

He paid for the three bottles and started to ride back to the Star Ranch.

Before he left town, Indian stopped and sent a telegram to Robert to let him know he was on his way back to Kansas City.

The telegraph operator said, "That's the second telegram I sent to Kansas City today."

Indian said, "Did you send one for Kent Eagle today?"

The telegraph operator said, "Now, how do you know that?"

"I saw him a while ago, and he said he sent a message to some of his men. Could I have a copy of his telegram? I'm going to be meeting up with his men."

"Well, I guess it would be all right."

So he made Indian a copy of the telegram, and Indian said, "I need to make one change in my telegram before you send it." Indian changed it to add, "Robert, you should see if you can meet with Al Beckett in Kansas City. He is working for the people we have been looking for."

Indian stayed at the ranch just long enough to pack his gear and get his two horses ready, and then Indian was on his way back to Kansas City.

CHAPTER TWENTY-THR EE

MEANWHILE, BACK IN KANSAS CITY

SERENE HAD BEEN A prisoner now for over three months, and for most of the time she had been kept in this small bedroom. The only time she was allowed out of her room was when they had meals, and once a week she was taken down the hall and allowed to take a bath.

Her room didn't have a lot in it; however, it did have a bed, chair, dresser, washbasin, water pitcher, washcloths and towels, and a chamber pot, which Al emptied and cleaned for her every day.

Al Beckett and Lightning Cole had treated her OK, except for one time, when Al slapped her when she was first captured.

Al had even gone out and bought her three new outfits of clothing, including underwear, which Serene found to be pretty amazing.

Al told her he had six sisters, and a very nice lady helped him get her clothes at the ladies' clothing store.

He even bought her shoes and stockings; maybe they weren't what she would have bought for herself, but they were comfortable, and she didn't have to keep wearing her cowboy boots every day.

Her captors had even been nice enough to put a lock on her bedroom door so she could have some privacy. They weren't worried about her escaping by going out through the only small window in her bedroom.

They were on the third floor in a building built on the side of a hill, which meant if she wanted to try to go out the window, she would have to fall some forty or fifty feet straight down on the rocks below her.

She couldn't cry out the window for help because there was nothing behind the building but trees.

They also had a lock on the outside of the door, so if someone came into their apartment, she couldn't come out.

As far as Serene knew, in the months they lived there, no one had ever been in their room.

When Al was out of the apartment, sometimes Lightning would let her out for a while so he had someone to talk with.

Serene learned that Lightning had spent his life as a gunfighter, since he was sixteen years old, and as a hired gun for whoever needed protection, or in some cases to scare homesteaders off.

He said, "It wasn't much of a life, although it paid a lot better than being a cowboy or a farmer."

He told Serene she was about the only girl he had ever had a conversation with.

It seemed his parents and their kids were on their way to California when they were attacked by Indians, and his parents and brothers were killed.

He escaped because he killed several Indians, and they decided it wasn't worth staying around to kill him or having more of their own killed. They already had almost everything his folks had that was worth stealing, including their horses, so they left him.

After the Indians left, he buried his folks and brothers and began walking somewhere; he said he had just turned sixteen at the time, and he had no idea where he was walking to. So he just kept walking.

He managed to find some homesteaders and stayed with them for a while until he found a wild horse.

Lightning said after he worked with the horse awhile, he was able to ride it, and he left and found his way into some little town in Kansas.

When he got to this town, some guy there was trying to show off to his friends how fast a draw he was with his gun, and when he saw Lightning ride into town he told him, "Either you have to fight me, or I'll just shoot you." All the while his friends kept egging him on.

"When he got off his horse, the young man drew his gun, but I drew mine quicker and I killed him.

"So that was the beginning of my new life. After his friends saw me draw, they said I was quicker than lightning. So that's how I got my name, Lightning.

"I had heard about the outlaws named Cole, so I took that for my last name. I became Lightning Cole. So far, I haven't found anyone quicker than I am. So I'm still living.

"Like I said, it's not much of a life."

Serene actually felt sorry for him, even though he was one of the men who had been holding her hostage.

She tried to tell Lightning that if he would help her to get home, she would pay him more money than he was being paid by the people he was working for.

Lightning said, "Ma'am, I would let you go right now, but my friend Al wouldn't like it. He'd raise a fuss. Then I'd have to shoot him. He's the only friend I have in the whole world. No, ma'am, I can't let you go."

"No, I understand you can't shoot your best friend, but maybe you can talk him into helping me, and I'd pay him too."

"I don't know, ma'am. Al's pretty funny about things like that. It can be pretty hard to get him to change his mind about who he works for. He says it ain't ethical, whatever that means.

"He says if you work for someone, you can't change sides. No, ma'am, I know he wouldn't do it."

"Lightning, you'd better lock me back up in my room before Al comes back. I wouldn't want you to get into trouble with your friend."

Serene started back to her room when Al came into the apartment and said, "Lightning, what's she doing out of her room?" "Well, I like to talk to her sometimes when you're gone, so I let her out of her room. She ain't trying to escape or nothing." "I don't want her out here when I'm not here!"

"Al, I don't know why you're making such a fuss."

"Our boss doesn't want her touched or molested in anyway. You got that, Lightning?"

Serene said, "It's all right. He's never touched me. Lightning just likes to talk to me. I'm sure he's lonesome staying here in this apartment month after month. I know I sure am."

Al responded, "OK, so he's been a perfect angel, but you're not to be out of you room when I'm gone."

Lightning said, "OK, Serene, you'll have to go back to your room."

Lightning opened the bedroom door, and Serene went back into her room without saying another word.

Lightning closed and locked the door to her room.

Serene heard Al and Lightning talking. She heard Al say, "I don't think we will have to keep her here much longer. I got a telegram today saying things will be finished in two days in Cuero. "The boss said he would send us another telegram in three days after the deal was finished. Then we could release her."

Serene wondered what that meant that "the deal would be finished in two days." She didn't have any idea what date it was now.

She did think it must be close to February 1, and that was when the bank would be foreclosing on her ranch. She thought that must be what the telegram was talking about.

In two days, her dad's fifty years of work to build the Star Ranch would belong to someone else.

Serene kept thinking, "One of these days, Indian will come crashing through the apartment door with his guns blazing and rescue her, and everything will be OK."

But in all these months, it never happened.

Serene didn't know how Indian could find her or be able to save her, but she knew somehow he would.

*****

Three days passed, and Al told Lightning he was going to the telegraph office to see if he had a telegram from their boss and warned him not to let Serene out of her room.

Indian had sent a telegram to Robert telling him about the message Kent Eagle had sent to his men in Kansas City. He told Robert that the name of the man the telegram was sent to was Al Beckett.

Robert spoke with the people working in the telegraph office at Union Station and told them he worked for the Pinkerton Detective Agency, and he was trying to locate a man named Al Beckett who was wanted for kidnapping a woman.

Robert said they had information the man would be receiving a telegram soon, and there would be twenty dollars in it if they could point the man out when he came to pick up the telegram. They said they would do that.

Robert sat across the room for two days, waiting for the signal when Al Beckett came to pick up his telegram.

Robert watched everyone who came to the telegraph office, and then late in the afternoon of the second day, the man working in the telegraph office waved at Robert as soon as a man left the counter.

Robert hurriedly went over to the telegraph office, and the clerk said, "That's Al Beckett."

Robert handed the clerk a Double Eagle coin and followed the man out of Union Station.

Robert tried not to get too close behind Al Beckett because he didn't want the man to see he was following him.

As the man walked along, he tore open the envelope, took out the telegram, and read it.

Then the man suddenly stopped, and Robert heard the man say, "Damn that no-good son of a bitch! I ain't killing no woman." As soon as Al said that, he looked around to see if anyone was around who might have heard him and decided no one was close enough to hear him. He then proceeded to walk on. Robert had ducked into a doorway, so Al didn't see him.

Arriving back at the apartment building, Al went up the stairs to the apartment and opened the door and found Lightning sitting at the table, staring off into space.

Robert entered the building in time to see Al going up to the third floor of the building, so he knew on what floor they were holding Serene.

Robert began ascending the stairs until he was on the third floor; then slowly Robert began listening at the door of each apartment, trying to hear anything he could to be sure he knew which apartment Serene was being held in.

It wasn't long before Robert heard the same man's voice he had heard on the street saying, "Lightning, can you believe that no- good son of a bitch has the nerve to send us a telegram telling us to kill Serene Star.

"Who in the hell does he think we are? Kidnapping her and holding her is one thing, killing her is something else."

Lightning said, "We ain't killing Serene Star, and if you think you're going to do what the boss told you, you're going to have to kill me first.

"I think you know you'll be dead if you try. I sure don't want to hurt you, Al. You're my best friend, but we're not killing Serene." "Lightning, we're not killing her. She's a nice lady. No, sir, I guess we'll have to go to Cuero, Texas, and kill Kent Eagle to keep him from hiring somebody to kill us."

Robert listened to every word Al Beckett said and decided to make sure they didn't change their minds about killing Serene.

Robert messed up his hair some and started pounding on their apartment door, yelling like he was drunk, "Alice, open up this damn door! You can't keep your husband out of our apartment. Come on, baby, let me in. You know I love you. You're my everything."

As Robert was saying this, he kept pounding on the door. Finally, Al said, "Go away you drunken fool. You're at the wrong apartment."

Robert didn't go away; he kept pounding on the door.

Al finally opened the apartment door, and when he did, Robert grabbed him and turned him around and held him with one arm around Al's neck while pointing his gun at Lightning.

Robert said, "Put your gun on the floor and step away from it! Where's Serene Star?"

Lightning put his gun on the floor and stepped away from it and said, "She's OK. She's in the bedroom."

Robert picked Al up off the floor, using the arm he was holding him with, and came inside the apartment. He told Lightning to open the bedroom door, "I want to see her myself to be sure she's all right."

Lightning opened the door, and Serene came out of the bedroom and saw Robert and said, "Thank God, you've found me." Robert said, "It took a long time to find you. Indian has been going crazy worrying about you."

Serene said, "Where is Indian? I thought he would be with you."

He's on his way back from Cuero after paying off your note at the bank. He found out who was holding you here by getting a telegraph operator to give him a copy of a telegram from Kent Eagle telling these two jokers to kill you."

"Is Indian all right? After he saw the telegram, he didn't do anything foolish, did he?"

"No, Serene, he didn't do anything foolish after he read the telegram. As soon as Indian knew who was holding you, he left to come back to Kansas City.

"I understand he did have to kill some gunman named Texas Tom Kent Eagle had sent to kill him."

"Oh, Robert, why or how did he do that?"

"It seems Eagle had gotten control of the Cuero bank and wasn't going to let anyone pay off your note, but Indian forced the bank manager to take the money and give him a receipt and the paid off note.

"Eagle didn't like that so he sent Texas Tom to kill Indian and get the receipt and the note back. He was like most people in our world. He wasn't as quick on the draw as Indian or as good a shot."

"Did Indian get hurt?"

"No, he's fine. He's coming to Kansas City as fast as he can get here to marry you, or as he said, if you're still willing to marry him."

"I'm still willing and waiting for him."

Robert took his arm from around Al's neck and said to Serene, "I don't know what we should do with these two: shoot them or turn them over to the authorities."

Serene said, "Robert, wait a minute, and I'll tell you what I want you to do with these two."

Al and Lightning both were holding their breaths, waiting to hear what Serene would tell Robert to do.

Robert asked, "OK, Serene, what do you want me to do with them."

Robert cocked the hammer of his revolver, waiting for Serene to answer. Al and Lightning too were waiting to hear what she would say.

Lightning considered if he should make a try for his gun lying on the floor in front of him.

Serene said, "Al, Lightning, I don't know how bad you two men may have been in your life, but except for one slap in the face Al gave me when you first captured me, you two have looked after me like I was a sister you really loved.

"Here's the deal. Robert can turn you over to the authorities, and you both can spend a long time in prison. Or you can come to work for me on my ranch for the next five years.

"You will be paid the same wages as the rest of my cowboys.

"If you run off, I'm not going to send someone after you. If you can live with breaking a promise to me then it will be on your conscience to live with for the rest of your life.

"What do you want to do? You have to tell me right now. It's one or the other."

Robert said, "If you want to have one other choice, you can try for your guns, but I wouldn't advise it. My trigger finger is ready to send you both to your Maker."

Al spoke first, "Miss Serene, we've been living with you for the past several months, and I think you're one of the nicest persons I ever met.

"I don't have any idea why you would make such an offer, but I would be honored to work for you."

Then Lightning spoke, "Miss Serene, you don't know it, but when Al told me Kent Eagle told us to kill you, I said I wouldn't let him do it if he even thought about it. I told my best friend in the world I would kill him if he tried.

"I'm like Al. I would be honored to work for you. I'd do anything for you. Like I told you, Al said if we work for somebody, we stay loyal to them. We never change sides."

Serene said, "OK, that's settled. You two are now working for the Star Ranch, and the first you job you have is to get to Cuero, Texas, and out to the Star Ranch."

Robert said, "OK, Lightning, pick up your gun so you can get ready to go to work in Texas."

Serene asked, "Al, do you have enough money to get to Texas?" Al replied, "I still have money left from what Kent Eagle gave me. We'll have to buy some horses, but we have our tack. No problem, if we don't have enough we can always rob somebody."

Serene said, "What?"

"I was just kidding, Serene. We wouldn't rob anybody."

CHAPTER TWENTY-FOUR

REUNION IN KANSAS CITY

NDIAN ARRIVED IN KANSAS City on April 1. He was dead tired and went directly to the hotel where Robert was staying.

When he got to the hotel, he asked for the room number of Robert Smiley and was told he was now in room six, located on the first floor.

Indian went to room six and heard someone talking; he knocked on the door, and Robert opened the door.

When Robert saw Indian, he grabbed him, picked him up, and gave his friend a huge hug. Then Robert sat him down inside his room.

Indian saw two ladies sitting in Robert's room, and Indian said, "Excuse me, Robert, I didn't know you were entertaining guests." Indian didn't recognize the women.

Robert said, "Indian, I would like to introduce you to my guests, Miss Serene Star and Miss Joan Sterling.

"Ladies, this worn-out thing is the famous trail boss, Mr. Indian Leader."

Indian did a double take at the two women and saw one was his Serene, all dressed up in big city clothes.

Indian said, "My God, you look beautiful, Serene. Wow! I never saw you dressed like this before."

Serene reached Indian, and he took her in his arms and held her as close as possible but not as close as he wanted to.

Serene said, "You can hold me tighter than this, Indian. I've been waiting a long time for this hug."

Indian then held her much tighter and said, "I love you so much, Serene. I'm so glad you're all right after being held a prisoner for so long. I've got lots of questions about you being kidnapped. Did the men holding you treat you all right? Let me take a real good look at you."

Indian released Serene from his arms because he wanted to take a long look at her from top to bottom and then back again.

Indian couldn't believe this beautiful woman was really going to marry him.

Serene said, "Indian, I want you to meet my best friend, Joan Sterling. She's come all the way from New York City to be my bridesmaid for our wedding."

Indian said, "I'm very glad to meet you. Serene must be a very good friend for you to come all the way from New York to be her bridesmaid."

Joan replied, "We made a pact a long time ago that when we got married we would each be the other's bridesmaid, so here I am." Indian said, "Joan, obviously since you are in his room you have already met my best friend, Robert Smiley. I want you to know he will be my best man."

Serene said, "Joan and I stopped by Robert's room to have a drink before going to dinner.

"Indian, I'm so happy you're here. You have no idea how much I missed you. I'm thrilled you're here and that we can all go to dinner together."

"Robert, where did you plan to have dinner tonight?"

"I thought we would have dinner here in the hotel restaurant, you know the Savoy Grill."

"Sounds good, but I'm not dressed to have dinner at such a fancy restaurant."

Serene said, "Indian, you look wonderful to me."

Robert added, "Indian, remember Kansas City is still a cow town. They're used to cowboys. You'll be just fine."

Indian replied, "Please let me get a room and get cleaned up some before we go to dinner."

Serene said, "OK, Indian, but don't take too long. We're all hungry."

"I won't be too long. It will give you folks a chance to finish your drinks."

Serene said, "I need a kiss before you go. It's been a long time." Indian took Serene into his arms and gave her a long, passionate kiss before leaving.

Indian checked into the hotel and took his things to the room. He gave himself a sponge bath, shaved, combed his hair, and put on the only clean clothes he had with him and hurried back to Robert's room.

Indian knocked on the door and Robert opened the door and said, "Well, cowboy, you look better. Are you ready to go to dinner?"

Before Indian could answer, Serene and Joan both shouted, "We're ready!"

Indian replied, "I guess I'm ready because the ladies must be really hungry because they seem really ready to go."

The four of them had a wonderful dinner at the Savoy Grill; the steaks were perfect, and they had a couple of bottles of very good wine.

Indian knew nothing about wine, but it seemed Joan knew a lot about them. So she chose the wine. Indian had to admit it went very well with their dinner.

Drinking wine was a totally new experience for him. He decided the folks back east knew something about living the good life.

After dinner, they returned to Robert's room where an interesting discussion took place regarding marriage.

Serene said, "Joan and my friends back east thought I was crazy coming back to Texas to live on a ranch out in the middle of nowhere, but I had my reasons."

Joan replied, "Well, I can see one of the reasons: he appears to be about six foot two and very handsome."

Indian said nothing; he was just busy turning red.

Robert said, "How about me? I'm even taller and better looking than Indian."

Joan laughed and said, "You're something, Robert, and you are even taller than Indian."

Joan put her right hand on Robert and said, "You know what, Robert? I might just marry you tomorrow. Then we could have a double wedding."

Robert said, "Joan, I can tell you, your parents would just love it if you married me and took me back to New York with you."

"Now, Robert, if I really married you and we went home to New York, my family would welcome you into the family."

"Joan, I can hear your dad say, 'Come on in here, Robert,' and as his son-in-law, he'd give me a job in one of his banks.

"Let me tell you, when my mother married my father and they returned to the Indian reservation, her parents told my mother as long as she was married to a white man, they never wanted to see her again.

"If it hadn't been for my grandfather, Chief Sequoia, who stood up for her by welcoming my father, my parents would have become outcasts in both the white and Indian world.

"Even then, there was one condition, and that was my father would have to become a teacher on the reservation. Then they would make him a member of the tribe. He agreed, and both of my parents teach at the reservation.

"Do you still think your rich parents and their friends would welcome you home if you were married to a half-breed? I think not."

Even though Joan knew he was right, she replied, "OK, Robert, if you don't want to marry me, you could have just said no."

Indian said, "Serene, we have a lot to talk about before we get married tomorrow."

Joan said, "I think since my heart has been broken by Robert not wanting to marry me, it would be better if you waited to talk things over until tomorrow morning. Indian looks pretty tired right now."

Indian said, "I think Joan has a point. I'm pretty well beat. How about it, Serene? Can we talk about everything in the morning?"

Serene replied, "I think that would be good. Indian, you can see me to my room."

Joan said, "I'll see you to your room, young lady. As your bridesmaid, it's my duty to see that you remain a good girl until you're wed. Then you can be a very bad girl."

The three of them laughed hard at Joan's statement, and Indian said, "Well, I'll give you a good-night kiss right here because I don't want to marry a bad girl, and I don't want you to become a problem for your bridesmaid."

Indian took Serene into his arms and kissed her good night. When the kiss was finished, Robert said, "Remember, girls, tomorrow I have to take Indian shopping so he looks presentable for the wedding. He can't be looking like he just finished a cattle drive, like he does right now."

Indian smiled as he said, "Thank you, my very dear friend, for all your kind attention."

After the girls left, Indian told Robert he was going to go to the front desk to make some arrangements for the wedding.

Robert said, "I'll be glad to go with you and help you if I can." "I think that would be good, since I've never been involved with making plans for a wedding. I'd love your company."

The two of them made their way to the front desk and found a lady who was working there.

She told Indian she could make some suggestions for his wedding.

The lady's name was Ida, and she said, "Since you will be leaving from the hotel to go to the city hall for your marriage licenses and your wedding ceremony, I would suggest you let me make arrangements for a carriage to take you to and from the hotel. You can't have your bride walking down these dirty walkways."

Indian replied, "That's sounds like a good idea. Don't you think so, Robert?"

"I certainly do, considering what I've heard about your bride's gown."

Indian said, "OK, Ida, would you please make arrangements for a carriage for us?"

"All right. I'll take care of it for you.

"Next, I want to book you into a brand-new suite we have just completed here at the hotel. It's a very special suite.

"We call it our 'Honeymoon Suite.' It's the first one west of the Mississippi River. I can tell you, your bride will be really excited about spending your wedding night there.

"It will always be a wonderful memory of your wedding day for both of you."

"How much is this honeymoon suite going to cost?"

"Only $25 a day, but if it will make you feel any better, we'll throw the nights in for free."

Indian and Robert couldn't keep from laughing at what Ida said.

Finally Indian said, "OK, that's sure a lot more than the four dollars a night I'm paying now."

"Well, it's a lot more room than the two rooms you have now, so look at it this way: it's only seventeen dollars more than what you're paying for your two rooms."

"OK, Ida. What else can you think of that we should do for our wedding?"

"Just a couple more things. You're going to need your wedding pictures taken, and you're in luck because we have the best photographer in Kansas City right here in our building."

Indian said, "I guess you're right. We will need a picture of our wedding day."

"OK, I'll take care of that for you.

"Now the only other thing I can think of is to make arrangements for your wedding dinner tomorrow night at our Savoy Grill. It is the best place in town for that, so I'll make arrangements for dinner for you.

"I'll have them chill a couple of bottles of French champagne for you and have our cook prepare a special dinner for you.

"How many people will be at your wedding dinner?" "Just four people, our wedding party."

"OK, I'll take care of all that for you, and when you are at your wedding, I'll have your and your bride's things moved from your rooms to the honeymoon suite.

"Let me be sure I have your bride's name right. It's Serene Star, right?"

"That's right, and thank you, Ida, so much. I really do appreciate your help."

"Well, you have a wonderful wedding and a wonderful life together. We've certainly got you started off on the right foot."

Robert said, "Well, cowboy, on your last night of freedom, do you want to have one last drink before going to bed? It will be your last chance to have a drink without having your wife's permission." "OK, Robert, one more drink, and then I've got to get to bed.

It's going to be a busy day tomorrow."

"Yeah, you better get some rest tonight. You'll be too busy tomorrow night."

CHAPTER TWENTY-FIVE

WEDDING DAY IN KANSAS CITY

THE NEXT MORNING, ROBERT was knocking on Indian's door before 7:00 a.m., and Indian could hear Robert saying,

"Come on, cowboy, rise and shine! We've got to go shopping to make you presentable for your wedding."

Indian opened the door and told Robert, "Come on, let's have some breakfast before we start shopping. I need coffee after that one drink-turned-into-six last night."

After breakfast, Indian and Robert went shopping at a very nice-looking men's store, where Indian was able to find everything Robert thought he needed to look presentable, as Robert kept telling him.

He found a very well-made, good-looking black suit; a fancy white shirt; a black silk neckerchief; black cowboy boots made by a new boot-maker named Lucchese; and a black Stetson hat. He was ready to get married now.

After Indian got dressed in his new outfit, he said, "You know, instead of going back to the hotel to change clothes. I'll just keep wearing these."

Arriving back at the hotel, he saw Serene and Joan coming into the lobby of the hotel looking for him.

Joan was dressed in a very nice-looking white dress; she looked lovely.

Then Indian took a good look at Serene. She looked like an angel in her wedding dress. It was white with fancy buttons and with ruffles on a very long full skirt, and she was wearing a small white hat with a peacock feather on it. Her gown and her hat set 188 off the color of her face, and her lovely brown eyes and long dark- brown hair.

Indian thought she was more beautiful than all those Greek goddesses he had read about.

One thing that made her even more beautiful was that when she saw Indian, a smile lit up her face and she said, "Wow, cowboy! You want to get married?"

Indian blushed and said, "Yes, ma'am, do you know a woman who'd marry an old cowboy like me?"

"Cowboy, the way you look, I'd marry you myself." "That's good, because you're the one I had in mind."

Robert said, "Ladies, ole Indian cleaned up pretty good, didn't he?"

Both Serene and Joan answered, "He sure did!"

Indian said, "Since we have this beautiful bride and lovely looking bridesmaid, I think we should go before the bride changes her mind."

Serene answered, "No chance, cowboy."

Indian asked at the desk if the rig Ida had made arrangements for was available, and he was told it was waiting for them at the front of the hotel.

The four of them walked outside the hotel and found waiting for them a team of white horses attached to a white carriage trimmed with gold stripes. with the carriage had four doors and a tan-colored top, with white fringe on the outside of the roof.

The driver had on a black top hat and black suit and wore white gloves. He opened the doors of the carriage—quite an impressive-looking carriage driver, to say the least. Indian and Robert were favorably impressed.

Indian tried to be causal about the whole thing and said, "Driver, do you know our destination?"

The driver replied, "Yes, sir. Miss Ida told me you were going to city hall to get married and then coming back to the hotel."

Indian said, "Thank you. We appreciate you looking after us." "It's my pleasure, sir."

The girls were giggling and trying not to be too loud about it.

Indian and Robert just stared at each other, trying not to join in giggling with the girls.

It didn't take very long for them to reach city hall. When they arrived, the driver got down, came back and opened the doors of the carriage, and helped the ladies out.

The driver said, "Mr. Leader, I'll be waiting right here for you when you're ready to go back to the hotel."

"Thank you, Driver. We'll be back in a few minutes."

The four of them made their way up the stairs to the front door and soon found the city clerk's office; as soon as they were inside, a man came to help them and said, "I believe you folks are here to get married, and you need a marriage license."

Indian said, "Yes, we are."

The clerk took down their names and filled out the licenses and said, "The judge across the hall will marry you."

Indian paid the two dollars for the license, and the four of them walked across the hall. Judge John Brown took one look at the four of them and said, "I'll bet you two want to get married and make everything legal, don't you?"

Indian and Serene said, "Yes, we do."

The wedding ceremony took only a few minutes, and the judge had all of them sign the wedding certificate. He gave a copy of it to Serene and said, "OK, Serene, you've got proof he married you. You can do with him whatever you want now."

Serene laughed and said, "I don't think you know Indian. He does what he wants to do."

Judge Brown said, "My young lady, that's what he used to do. From now on he'll be doing what you want him to."

The four of them laughed, and Indian said, "Thank you, Judge."

They returned to the hotel, and Indian said, "Serene, I have to go to my room. I forgot something I have for you."

Indian went to his room and found that all his things had been moved to the honeymoon suite, so he marched down to the front desk and told the man working there that he needed to get the key to his new room.

The clerk said, "Here you are, Mr. Leader. We certainly hope you and your bride enjoy your new suite."

As Indian turned to go to his new room, Serene and Joan came to the front desk, and Serene said, "Indian, someone has taken all my things out of my room."

Indian smiled but before he could say anything, Serene said, "I don't know what you're smiling about! Someone has taken all my clothes out of my room!"

"It's all right, Serene. The hotel has moved all our things to a new room. I forgot to tell you we have a new suite. I was just getting the key for it. Come on, and we'll go together and check it out."

Serene replied, "I wish you had told me, so I could have straightened up my things so they could have moved them easier." Indian took her hand, and together they began walking to their new suite.

Joan said, "You two go ahead. Robert and I are going to have some coffee in the lobby bar."

On arriving at their new suite, they found a gold-colored plaque on the door, with the name of the suite on it "Honeymoon Suite."

Indian unlocked and opened the door, not having any idea what they were in for with a honeymoon suite.

The first thing they saw was that it had the largest bed Indian and Serene had ever seen. When Serene looked around for her clothes, she found there was a small little room with her clothes hanging in it. Serene knew about closets from living in the east but had never seen one anywhere in west.

While she was checking out the closet, Indian opened another door and shouted to Serene, "Come here and see what's in this room!"

Serene joined him and said, "My God! We have a bathroom with a tub and a toilet."

Indian was busy checking out this thing Serene called a "toilet." He found it had a wooden seat and a bowel below the seat with water in it.

Serene came over as Indian was staring at the water in the bowl; she pushed a small lever on the back of the toilet, and the water in the bowl swirled around in the bowl and went out through a small hole in the bottom of the bowl. Then fresh water began to fill up the bottom of the bowl.

Serene said, "I never expected to see a real toilet here in a hotel in Kansas City."

Indian asked, "You mean this thing replaces the chamber pots? What do you think they will think up next?"

"Oh, Indian, we're living in an age where everything we used to do is going to change for the better."

Serene loved their suite!

Indian found his saddlebags and looked around until he found the small box he had been looking for. Then he handed it to Serene and said, "Serene, I plumb forgot to bring this to our wedding ceremony."

Serene opened the box and found a beautiful gold wedding band. She said, "Indian, you have to put it on my finger to make me a married woman."

Indian took the ring, placed it on the third finger of her left hand, and said, "Serene, I love you now and always, and this ring is a token of my love for you."

He took her in his arms and gave her a kiss and said, "We should rejoin Joan and Robert."

"I guess we have to, but I'd rather stay here in our suite with you, my love."

They spent the rest of the afternoon talking about the adventures they had on the trail drive and the search Robert and Indian had for Serene.

Serene told them about how she was treated during the months she was held hostage.

Then they talked about what each of them wanted in their lives in the future.

Indian told Serene he had made arrangements to have wedding pictures taken so they could always remember this day.

When they arrived at the photographer's studio, he had everything ready for them.

He took the standard picture of the bride and groom and then said, "I would like to suggest we also take a picture of the four of you. That way, you will have a record of your bridesmaid and your best man."

Serene said, "I think that's a brilliant idea. I've never heard about anyone ever doing that. Have you, Joan?"

Joan replied, "No, not even in New York or Boston, but I know when I get married, I want to have a picture with my wedding party."

The photographer said, "Well, I believe in the future everyone will be taking more pictures at their wedding.

So they had a picture taken of the four of them.

Now it was time to go to Indian's special wedding dinner that Ida had planned for them.

When they arrived at the Savoy Grill, the waiter said, "Oh, you must be Mr. and Mrs. Leader and your wedding party. We have a wonderful dinner planned for you.

"First, we start with champagne and a small salad of greens, tomatoes, and green onions.

"For your main course, we have fresh Maine lobster with boiled potatoes, and for dessert, there's a special wedding cake made for you. It's a white cake with white icing, with a bride and groom on it, which you can take as a visual reminder of your wedding day."

Indian said, "It sounds wonderful."

They began by pouring champagne into some very beautiful glasses made for serving it.

Their salad was great; it had some type of topping which Indian and Robert had never tasted before.

When they brought their lobsters, Indian and Robert looked at the lobsters with no idea of how they were supposed to eat them, but Serene said to the waiter, "Please take them out of the shell for all of us."

The waiter removed the meat from the four lobster shells with ease as Indian and Robert watched in awe.

After the lobster's meat had been removed from its shell, Indian and Robert enjoyed eating it very much; it was their first experience of eating shell fish.

Joan said, "I never expected to have lobster in Kansas City. I guess with the railroad coming from Boston and New York, you will be able to get anything we have on the East Coast."

Lastly came their wedding cake, and Serene and Joan were very impressed with the decorations the baker had made on it.

Serene said, "I wish the photographer was here to take a picture of our beautiful cake so I could look at it along with our wedding pictures."

The waiter said, "Ma'am, you will have the little statue of the bride and groom to take with you to remind you of your wedding cake."

Serene replied, "Yes, thank you. That will be nice."

After they served the wedding party their cake and coffee, Indian said, "We would like to share our wedding cake with the rest of your diners eating here tonight, so please give a piece of our cake to them."

The waiter said, "Yes, sir. I will be glad to do that. I know the other diners will appreciate it."

All the diners were served the wedding cake, and as they were leaving the restaurant, they all stopped by to congratulate the bride and groom.

Finally, the wedding dinner was finished, and the last of the champagne had been drunk when Indian said, "I think we need to go to bed, don't you, Serene?"

Serene smiled and said, "Well, I am getting pretty tired." Robert broke in and said, "I think it's been a pretty exciting few days for you two old married people, so you better waddle your way to bed so you will be rested enough tomorrow."

Then Joan added, "Yes, you two do look really taxed. You better get to bed!"

Robert and Joan began laughing as Indian and Serene both got up from the table and said, "Good night, you young folks."

Robert and Joan also left the table and started walking hand in hand out the front door of the hotel as Indian and Serene made their way to their suite.

Indian was soon undressed and in bed; Serene was in the bathroom, and when she came out, she was wearing a pink French silk nightgown. Indian took one look at her in the nightgown, reached for her hand, and pulled her into bed.

They spent the rest of the night finally satisfying the desires they both felt when they were kissing in the chuck wagon so many months ago.

CHAPTER TWENTY-SIX

ANOTHER DAY IN KANSAS CITY

THE NEXT MORNING, INDIAN and Serene looked at the clock, and it told them it was now ten thirty.

They looked into each other's eyes, and Indian said, "Good morning, my love. How did you sleep?"

"Like I never slept before in my life. I can't believe how relaxed I am. I feel wonderful. How about you?"

"You know I feel the same way. It was wonderful, and the sleep wasn't bad either."

It was Serene's turn to turn red in the face, and then she said, "I never thought it would feel so good. It was wonderful. Wow!"

"You're right as always, my dear wife."

It was the first time Indian had ever said "my wife." He liked the sound of it.

"No, my husband, I'm not always right, just most of the time." Indian asked, "Do you know when Joan is planning on going home? By the way, where is her home?"

"She doesn't have a date yet for going home because we didn't know when you would be back in Kansas City and then when our wedding was going to be.

"You asked where her home is—her family has a home in New York City, another one in Boston, and a summer home in Maine."
"Wow, that's a lot of homes. What does her father do?"

"You know what Robert said about her daddy? He could make him the president of one of his banks. Her family does own banks in New York City and Boston.

"Plus the family is in shipping, mining, and trading companies and is part owner of Lloyds of London.

"They are one of the richest families in America." "What is this Lloyd's of London?"

"It's a company that insures ships and their cargo. It was started in the late 1600s, and one of the men who started it was one of Joan's father's great-great-grandfathers, a Lord somebody. It was before the family moved to America.

"So, they have always been rich? That's some family!"

"Yes, Indian. It is some family. Joan and her one brother are the only heirs to all those businesses and the money."

"Well, my love. I've never known anyone like that. What kind of a guy is her brother?"

"He's very nice and good-looking. He once asked me to marry him. I didn't love him so I told him, 'no,' and that I was going back home to Texas to work with my dad."

Indian said, "Good for me."

"Now you know just how lucky you really were to get me."

"I knew I was lucky to get you before, but now I know just how lucky I am."

Serene said, "I think we'd better get up and see if Joan has made any plans to go home yet."

Indian replied, "OK, if we have to. I would rather stay in bed and make love with you all day."

"Maybe tomorrow, cowboy. Right now I want to use the bathroom and take a bath before we get dressed."

Reluctantly, Indian agreed that they owed it to their best friends to see what they were doing.

After Serene and Indian were bathed and dressed, they set out to find Joan and Robert, because the last time they saw them the two of them they were going out of the hotel.

They looked all around the hotel and didn't find them.

Then Serene went to Joan's room and knocked on the door. It took quite a while for Joan to open the door, and when she did, Serene saw she was still in her nightgown.

Joan rubbed her eyes and said, "Serene, come in here."

Serene went inside Joan's room and saw that the bed was a mess, and the clothes she wore yesterday were strewn all over her room.

Serene asked, "Joan, are you all right? I was your roommate for a long time, and I never saw you leave your clothes in such a mess."

"Serene, you wouldn't believe the night Robert and I had."
"Don't tell me you went to bed with Robert?"

"No, we didn't go to bed with each other. I tried, but he wouldn't do it. I got drunk after we went to some shows and saloons. I kept drinking all night.

"Then Robert had to get in a fight with two guys who were trying to get me to go with them. One of the guys tried to put his hand up my dress, and Robert flattened him.

"Then the second guy hit Robert on the head with a bottle, and that made Robert mad, so he knocked the second guy out.

"Just then, the first guy got up and took a swing at Robert. Robert then knocked out the guy's front teeth and threw him through a window and picked up the second guy and threw him through another window.

"It was unbelievable. I've never seen anything like it." "Well, how come your clothes are all over the room?"

"Robert brought me back to my room, and I tried to seduce him. I started taking off my clothes and throwing them at him."

"What did Robert do?"

"He laughed at me and told me I needed to go to bed and get some sleep. When I didn't have anything left on to throw at him, he picked me up in one arm turned down my bed covers with his other arm, and laid me gently into bed.

"You know what he said to me?" "No, Joan. What did he say to you?"

"He said, 'Joan you be a good girl and get some sleep, and you'll be feeling a lot better in the morning.'"

"What did you do then?"

"I kissed him, and he kissed me back. Then he said, 'That was a good night kiss. Now go to sleep.' Then he closed the door and left me."

"It sounds to me like he was a real gentleman."

"Yeah, he was, but it didn't make me feel like I was very much of a desirable woman. When he picked me up and put me in my bed, he just left me lying there, stark naked."

"Joan, I don't believe you! You don't know how lucky you were not to have been really taken advantage of by acting that way. I'm sure it was just too much to drink that caused you to act like that."

"You're half right, Serene. I had too much to drink. That was part of it. The other half was that I really wanted him to make love to me.

"I think I was thinking about you doing it with Indian, and I felt like I was getting left out of a natural part of life.

"The truth is, I'm really attracted to Robert. He's a great-looking man, and he's smart. He acts like he's not, but he is. Now I don't know how I'm going to face him. What do I say to him? Do I apologize for throwing myself at him or what?

"Other than my father, when I was a baby, no man has ever seen me naked and not many of my girlfriends, either. I'm really embarrassed. What do I do now?"

"I think the best thing you can do, Joan, is get dressed and go see if we can find Indian and Robert to see if Robert has anything to say about last night. If I know cowboys, he's not going to say anything about what happened last night to you or anybody else.

"Cowboys have some kind of a code. They don't talk about things like what happened with you last night or tell it to any of their friends. So get dressed while I straighten up your room a bit, and let's go find the guys."

Joan got dressed, and she and Serene walked down to the lobby and found Indian and Robert sitting in the lobby bar, drinking coffee.

When they arrived, Robert said, "Good morning, or I guess I should say, good afternoon. Would you ladies like some coffee?"

Joan answered, "I would love some coffee, Robert."

Robert got up from the table and pulled out a chair for Joan as Indian did the same for Serene. Then Robert went to find two more cups and another pot of coffee.

When Robert returned with the cups and coffee, he poured coffee for each of the girls and asked them if they would like to have something to eat.

Both of them told him no; they just needed some coffee right now.

Serene said, "Maybe I would like to have something to eat after we have a chance to drink our coffee."

Robert replied, "You ladies go ahead and enjoy your coffee. Indian and I are a full pot ahead of you."

Indian asked, "Joan, what did you and Robert do after we went to bed? We saw you leaving the hotel. I hope Robert didn't lead you astray here in the big city."

Joan had just taken a big swallow of her coffee when Indian asked his question. She started choking, coughing, and spitting out her coffee, but before she could recover from choking to answer Indian's question, Robert said, "We just took a little walk around town. I wanted to show Joan how beautiful the stars are here in the west."

Indian asked Joan if she was all right, and she told him, "Yes." She just got choked on her coffee. She said, "It happens sometimes when I'm drinking coffee."

He was glad she was all right.

Serene asked, "Joan, have you thought about when you will be going home?"

"Serene, I think I'm going to leave tomorrow. I have stayed longer than I thought I would. Is that OK with you, Serene?"

"Sure it is. I would love for you to come to see my ranch in Texas, but I think you'd better wait until we get a train coming our way. I don't think you're up to traveling the way we have to go home."

Robert said, "Joan, don't you go back east by going to Chicago?"

"Yes, why do you ask?"

"I've always wanted to go to Chicago, and if you would like to have some company, I would like to go with you that far."

Indian said, "I think that's a very good idea. I hate to think about Joan going from Kansas City to Chicago by herself. There are some pretty rough hombres who ride the trains from here to Chicago."

Joan said, "Robert, if you have time, I would love to have you go with me. You can look after me and keep me safe from, as Indian said, 'those rough hombres,' whoever they are."

Robert said, "Good. We can go over to the station and get our tickets for tomorrow whenever you are ready."

After the girls finished their coffee, Joan said, "I'm ready to go to the train station whenever you're ready, Robert."

"Let's go, 'cause if you're waiting for me, you're backing up." Indian asked, "What the hell does that mean, Robert?"

"I don't know. It's something that just popped into my head." Joan said, "Don't let too many more statements like that pop into your head."

The four of them laughed; then Robert and Joan got up from the table and left to go to the train station.

Indian and Serene decided to go have something for lunch. Indian said, "I'm going to have to have some fuel if we plan on another night like we had last night."

Serene replied, "Then by all means, let's get you fueled up because I'm certainly looking forward to another night just like last night."

Indian and Serene went to the dining room for lunch.

As Robert and Joan were walking to the train station, Joan said, "Robert, I want to apologize for the way I acted last night."

"No need to apologize. I had a great time."

"Robert, I certainly am ashamed of what I did. I guess I had too much to drink. However, I am really attracted to you, but I have no excuse for my actions."

"Joan, you don't have to be ashamed. Nothing bad happened."

"I'm glad you didn't think anything bad happened. I guess you have girls taking their clothes off and throwing them at you all the time."

"No, they never did. Joan, you have no idea how hard it was for me not to make love with you. There were three reasons I didn't:

"First, you would have hated me in the morning.

"Second, even worse, you would have hated yourself even more in the morning. I couldn't have you hating yourself. It was going to be bad enough you hating me."

"OK, Robert, but what was the third reason?"

"Because you're not the kind of girl who goes around making love with a bunch of men. You're the girl who comes to bed on her wedding night, ready to give herself to the man you'll be making love with all of your life."

"Thank you, Robert, for doing the thinking for both of us. At least now I know you weren't repulsed by the sight of my naked body, and you did want to make love with me."

"My dear Joan, I want you to know I'll hold the picture of your naked body in my mind the rest of my life."

"Do you know, Robert, I am in love with you? And I want you to be the man I'd give my body to on my wedding night."

"The truth is, Joan, I've loved you from the first moment I met you, but you know what I told you. It could never work because I'm a half-breed."

"Let me work on that, Robert. You don't know how I can wrap my father around my little finger, and I can get my mother and brother to help me get what I want."

"I think you would have to be a miracle worker to sell me to your father."

"Watch me!"

They purchased their tickets, not just to Chicago but all the way to New York City.

They never told Indian and Serene that Robert was not only going to Chicago with Joan, but he was going on to New York City to meet her family because she had decided she was marrying him.

The following day Robert and Joan boarded their train for Chicago, and Indian and Serene left on a train to Baxter Springs, Kansas.

CHAPTER TWENTY-SEVEN

COMING HOME TO THE STAR RANCH

NDIAN AND SERENE BOUGHT a buggy and a team of horses from Buddy Thompson when they arrived in Baxter Springs. Indian had left his horses, Prince and Captain, with Buddy to take care of when he took the train to Kansas City.

After they loaded Serene's trunk and Indian's valise, saddle, and tack into the back of the buggy, they didn't have much room left in the rear of the buggy.

Serene was very impressed with Indian's horses when he told her they wouldn't have to tie them to the buggy for them to follow them on the trip.

All Indian had to do was to tell Prince and Captain, "Come with me," and they would follow right behind the buggy. When the buggy stopped, they would stop, and they stayed right with them.

Indian planned to stop and see his parents when they got to the Cherokee Indian Reservation, which they arrived at the following day.

Indian's folks were thrilled to see Indian and to meet Serene. They loved her the first moment they saw her and told her she was the woman Indian needed to make his life complete.

Serene asked them to come and live on the ranch with them, but they told Serene, "As much as we would like to live next to Indian and you, we are getting pretty old, and it would be a long hard trip for us."

They would also have to leave their lifelong friends and their church, which they didn't want to do, because they would miss both their friends and their church.

Indian's mother said, "I couldn't leave my garden and my little house. Besides, I heard the earth isn't as good in Texas for growing my garden, and I love my garden."

When Indian and Serene left the next day, the four of them had tears in their eyes after the hugging and kissing was over. None of them knew if they would ever see each other again.

It took another three weeks for Indian and Serene to arrive at the Star Ranch.

Serene was happy to see her home again because she hadn't been sure it was going to be her home anymore with the threat of foreclosure on her dad's loan.

Indian and Serene met with Lloyd to see how thing had been on the ranch. They learned that all their crew had made it safely home, including Granny Hayes, who stayed to do the cooking at the ranch.

Indian asked Lloyd if they had had any trouble with rustlers while they had been gone.

He said, "No, we haven't had any trouble except the normal things you would expect to have running a ranch the size of the Star Ranch.

Indian said, "That's good. How about Kent Eagle? Has he been around the ranch at all?"

"As I told you, before you came back and paid off the note, he was here several times looking around and asking if the crew working here would stay on when he took over the ranch.

"Everyone told him they needed a job, and if he took over the ranch, we would all consider staying on. After you paid the note off, he hasn't been back."

Indian said, "Serene, I'm going into town to see what's happened since we've been gone. I have to find out what Eagle has been up to."

"Indian, I don't want you going into town by yourself. I want to have my husband around a long time."

"You know I can take care of myself, Serene. I don't need anybody looking after me."

"I know you can, but I still want you to take at least one person with you."

"OK, I'll take your friend, Lightning, with me. It sounds to me like he's been a paid gunman in the past.

"Lloyd, where do you have Lightning and Al working today?" "The two of them are cleaning up some equipment behind the bunkhouse."

Indian kissed Serene and said, "We'll be back for supper, love. See you then."

Indian walked to the rear of the bunkhouse and found Al and Lightning cleaning up some equipment, just as Lloyd told him they were.

Indian introduced himself to Al and Lightning and said,

"You know, of course, if I had my way, you would be in jail in Kansas City. However, since my wife is your champion, you're working here.

"I'm going into town to see if I can find your old boss, Kent Eagle. I don't know what will happen when I find him, so Serene wants me to take some men with me.

"I told her I would take one man with me and wonder if either of you two men would like to go with me?"

Both Al and Lightning shouted they wanted to go.

Indian said, "Here's what I think. I want Lightning to go with me since I understand you're the fastest draw with your gun.

"Al, I want you to get your gun and bring along a rifle and stick with Serene because if Eagle finds out she's home, he may come here and try to kill her. I know you had orders from him to kill her before, so I think he will try it again. Al, don't let that happen."

Before Indian and Lightning left the ranch, Indian rode over to where Lloyd was working and said, "Lloyd, I'm expecting you may have trouble while I'm gone. So get all our men armed, just in case I'm right. I've asked Al to get his weapons and stay with Serene. She's not going to like it, but if Kent Eagle finds out she's alive, he'll be coming here trying to kill her."

Lloyd told him he would get all their men armed, just in case. When Indian and Lightning arrived in town, their first stop was at the sheriff's office, and they found a note on the door reading: Sheriff Killed. Office Closed.

Their next stop was at the saloon where Indian asked the bartender to pour them a couple of shots of whiskey.

The bartender set down two small glasses and started to pour them a drink, when Lightning said, "No whiskey for me. I don't drink, so if you have some sarsaparilla, I'd have that."

The bartender said, "No problem," and poured Indian his whiskey; then he got a larger glass and poured Lightning his sarsaparilla.

Indian asked the bartender, "What happened to the sheriff?" "He got shot in the back about two weeks ago, and it was several days before anybody found his body."

"I'm sorry to hear that. As you know, I only saw him one time, but he seemed like a decent man."

"Yeah, he was. He was working on a couple of killings, and some people say he was about to arrest somebody for them when he was killed."

"Who else was killed?"

"The sheriff was trying to find the killer of two ranchers. You wouldn't know them. They just had small outfits bordering the Double Eagle Ranch."

Indian said, "Lightning, I think we should ride out and talk to the widows about what happened to their husbands."

Indian asked, "Bartender, your name is Sam, isn't it? "Yes, it is."

"Sam, before we ride out to the ranches, do you know if these ranchers had wives?"

"They do as far as I know. At least I heard the preacher say they did when he was trying to take up a collection to help them out."

"You don't know the name of the two ranchers who were killed, do you?"

"Sure do, their names were Chuck Finley and Dan Smith."

"It's strange to me that these two ranchers whose land adjoins the Double Eagle Ranch were both killed, and, Sam, you said the sheriff was killed near there too. Is that right?"

"Yeah, that's right. The only one who wasn't killed out in that same area was Mr. Wilson, the president of the bank. He was killed a little way from his home."

"I hadn't heard Mr. Wilson had been killed."

"I guess he was killed on his way home. When he didn't show up for supper on time, his wife went looking for him and found his body. I felt really sorry for her. She had a new baby girl just two days before Mr. Wilson was killed."

"That's really tough. Sorry to hear that. Sam, I think I know who's behind all these killings. Who would I see about giving my information to?"

"Hell, everybody in the county knows who's behind them. It's Kent Eagle, but nobody can prove it. And there's nobody willing to try to do anything about it."

"They're all afraid to say anything. If you two weren't the only ones in the saloon, I wouldn't say anything either."

"Sam, who could I talk to that hires or appoints the sheriff?"

"I believe you would need to talk to the county commissioner, Mike Swift. He runs the general store across the street."

"Thanks, Sam. We'll go talk to him."

Indian and Lightning walked across the street to the general store, and Indian asked to speak to Mike Swift and was told he was working in his office in the back of the store.

The clerk said, "You fellows can go on back to his office."

Indian and Lightning walked to the back through a storeroom and found Mike Swift's office and went in. Mr. Swift said, "What can I do for you men?"

Indian said, "My name is Indian Leader, and this is Lightning Cole. I'm Serene Star's new husband, and I think we can help you with the four killings that have taken place recently."

"That would be a good thing, but what makes you think you can help?"

Indian said, "Commissioner Swift, in the past I was a deputy sheriff for St. Louis County, Missouri, and the man I suspect is responsible for these killings is Kent Eagle."

"What makes you think so?"

Indian reached in his pocket and took out the telegram which had been sent to Al Beckett telling him to get rid of the item he was holding for him, and signed KE.

Commissioner Swift read the copy of the telegram and said, "So what was the item Al Beckett was holding for him?"

"Serene Star. Two men kidnapped Serene for Kent Eagle, and they were holding her for him. They were told they would keep her for only a few days, then let her go. You know, kind of like a joke.

"They wouldn't kill her. They let her go, and then they told Serene and me all about it. One of the men holding her was Lightning Cole."

Lightning Cole quickly picked up on what and how Indian changed the truth and said, "Yeah, my best friend, Al, and I took her and held her for a few days.

"When Mr. Eagle told us in his telegram to get rid of the item we were holding for him, he meant for us to kill her. When we took her, we thought he was going to marry Serene, not kill her."

Commissioner Swift asked, "So what do you want me to do about him? I'm a storekeeper, and why do you think he killed these people?"

"The same reason he had Serene kidnapped. He wanted to get control of all the ranches around his property because he thinks the railroad is coming through this area, and he thinks he can make a lot of money selling them the land."

"Indian, since I'm the county commissioner, I know the railroad is talking about a line coming through somewhere in our area, but they don't even know where the line will be or when they are going to build it.

"So let's get down to it. What do you want me to do to bring the guilty party to justice?"

"Appoint me sheriff and Lightning Cole and Al Beckett as deputies, and we'll take care of it."

"That I can and will do right now. Come along with me, and I'll get you both sworn in."

Mike Swift took the keys to the sheriff's office out of his desk, and the three of them went over to the sheriff's office. Mike unlocked the door, found the badges for the sheriff and two deputies, and handed the keys to the office to Indian.

Then he pinned the sheriff's badge on Indian and a deputy sheriff's badge on Lightning and said, "Repeat after me, using your own name: I, whatever your name is, hereby swear to faithfully uphold the laws of DeWitt County, Texas, to the best of my ability, so help me God."

After Mike finished swearing them in, he said, "Indian, you can swear in your other deputy. Right now, I have to get back to my store."

Indian said to Lightning, "Deputy, let's ride out and talk to the two widows of the ranchers who were killed and see if we can talk to Mrs. Wilson."

The last thing in the world Lightning Cole ever thought he would be was a lawman, but since he was a lawman now, he planned to do everything he could to be a good one.

After Indian and Lightning spoke with Mrs. Finley and Mrs. Smith, they discovered that both told them the same story.

Kent Eagle had made offers to their husbands to buy their ranches. They both told him they didn't want to sell their ranches.

After their husbands had been killed, Kent Eagle came back a few days later and offered to buy the ranches from their widows for half of what he had offered to their husbands.

They both told him no. They said they didn't have anywhere to go, but he told them he could wait since they had bank loans coming due and he could buy their ranches for a lot less when they couldn't make the payments.

When Indian and Lightning talked to Mrs. Wilson, she told them her husband was in the process of raising enough money to pay off Kent Eagle and get him out of the bank.

Mrs. Wilson said, "My husband hated Eagle and the things he made him do. He was scared Eagle would kill him after he let the loan be paid off on the Star Ranch."

She said her husband told her Kent Eagle was obsessed with marrying Serene Star and owning her ranch, and if he couldn't have her and the ranch, he swore to kill her.

Indian thanked her for her help and said, "We're going to do everything possible to see your husband's murderer is brought to justice."

She replied, "When you kill Kent Eagle, my husband will have his justice."

When they left Mrs. Wilson's house, Lightning said, "I think if I was Kent Eagle, he'd better never turn his back on one of those widows. Otherwise, they are going to pay him back in lead."

Indian replied, "Now, that would be real justice!"

Then Indian said, "I think we better be riding back out to the ranch and make sure we have enough men there to fight off Eagle and his men if they try to kill Serene."

Indian and Lightning began pushing their horses into a run back to the Star Ranch.

Before they arrived, they could see smoke coming from the ranch and continued running their horses as fast as they could go.

Indian shouted to Lightning, "We better slow up so we can take a look at what's going on before we ride right into the middle of a shoot-out."

They kept running their horses until they had a clear view of the ranch buildings.

Indian could see one side of the house burning, and shooting was still going on between people in the house and cowboys out behind the cookhouse and the bunkhouse.

Indian told Lightning, "You take the men behind the bunkhouse, and I'll go after the ones behind the cookhouse."

Lightning turned his horse toward where the men were firing from behind the bunkhouse, and Indian turned his horse toward the cookhouse.

When Lightning was in a position where he could shoot at the men behind the bunkhouse, he found a tree that offered a little bit of cover. He stepped off his horse with his rifle and began firing at those men.

His first shot dropped one man; his second shot hit a second man, and he went down.

Then, the other four men began running for their horses, and Lightning hit one more of the men before they could get to their horses. He kept firing until the last three men rode off away from the ranch.

Moments after Lightning started firing at the men behind the bunkhouse, Indian started shooting at the five men hiding behind the cookhouse.

Indian's first two shots dropped two of the men, and the other three headed for their horses. Indian continued shooting and hit two more of the men, but they were still able to get on their horses and ride off.

Indian made his horse step back and began riding toward the house when someone fired a shot in his direction; a bullet passed near his left ear.

Indian turned his horse back toward where the shot came from, and he saw Kent Eagle and another man turn their horses and take off in a dead run.

Indian reined up his horse and started back toward the house to see if Serene was all right.

Before Indian got to the house, he saw the bodies of two of their men lying on the ground, and then he saw the house was totally engulfed in flames.

Indian began shouting for Serene, and then he saw her, Al, Lloyd, and Granny Hayes running from the house.

Indian got off his horse and ran to Serene.

He saw some of her clothes were on fire, so he quickly grabbed her and pulled her down to the ground.

Then he began rolling her around on the ground, and at the same time he took handfuls of dirt and patted it on the flames on her clothes.

When he saw the flames were all out, he held her as close as he could and she said, "I'm OK, I think."

By this time the other three people from the house were standing around them, waiting to be sure Serene was all right.

Indian got up from the ground and offered his hand to Serene. She took his hand, and he pulled her up. Then he held her in his arms and said, "Serene, are you sure you're not badly burned?" "I don't think I am. I know right now, I'm pretty covered with dirt from the top of my head down to my boots."

Then all the folks from the house put their arms around both of them.

Lightning rode up and asked, "Is everybody OK?"

Serene looked up at Lightning and saw his badge and asked, "Lightning, what are you doing wearing a badge?"

Then she looked back at Indian and saw his badge and said, "Why do you have on the sheriff's badge?"

"My love, it's because someone has to do something about Kent Eagle and his men since everybody else is afraid to. I'm wearing the sheriff's badge because right now, I am the sheriff.

"The man who was sheriff of DeWitt County was killed along with two of your neighbors who owned small ranches next to the Double Eagle, and your banker, Mr. Wilson."

Serene asked, "What are you going to do, Indian?"

"We're going to try to arrest Kent Eagle and his men, but I guess if we can't, we'll have to kill them."

"Indian, I love you so much. It was a good thing you and Lightning got here when you did because I'm sure they would have killed all of us.

"I'm sorry you're the one who has to go after Kent Eagle and his men, but I know you have to do something about him or he will never leave us alone."

Indian said, "Al, I want you to go with us after Eagle and his men."

Then he pinned a deputy sheriff's badge on Al and said, "Al, do you swear to uphold the laws of DeWitt County, Texas, to the best of your ability?"

Al replied, "Well, I guess I do. I've already got the badge.

"You know you people are crazy, making Lightning and me deputy sheriffs. We're the least likely people to become lawmen that I know."

Indian said, "I think you and Lightning will do just fine, and we'll clean up this county as soon as we take care of Kent Eagle and his men."

Then Indian turned to Serene, Lloyd, and Granny Hayes and said, "It doesn't look like there is much of the house left, but you might want to see if you can salvage anything.

"I'm sorry we lost two men. Lloyd, where are the rest of our men?"

Lloyd answered, "I had them working on the east range today, checking on the cattle to be sure they had enough water or if we're going to have to move them closer to the creek near the house. So they should be all right."

Indian told Al to get his horse because they were going after Eagle and his men.

Al got a horse that belonged to one of the men who came with Eagle and mounted up and told Indian he was ready to go.

Before Indian got on his horse, he gave Serene a kiss and told her he'd see her as soon as they finished with Eagle.

The three of them rode off in the direction of the Double Eagle Ranch.

When they arrived there, they found only one man standing by the corral, and as soon as he saw them coming, he put his hands in the air and just stood there waiting for them.

Indian said, "Lightning, you and Al stay back. This may be a trick."

Lightning and Al stopped their horses and pulled out their rifles as Indian rode up to where the man was standing.

Indian said, "Where's Eagle and the rest of the men?"

The man answered, "Most of the men rode off saying they weren't going to have anything else to do with the boss. They said he's gone crazy.

"Eagle and his hired gunman went riding off in the direction of Cuero. I was just going to get a horse and leave the county and was never coming back. Is that all right with you, Sheriff?"

"OK, get a horse and get out of DeWitt County, or the next time I see you, it will be either in jail or boot hill, got that?"

"Yes, sir."

Indian turned his horse toward Cuero and told Lightning and Al to follow him.

He said, "The guy told me Eagle and his gunslinger rode off in the direction of Cuero, while the rest of his men hightailed it out of the county."

The three of them rode as fast as they could to Cuero, and when they arrived, they found Main Street was empty. No one was to be seen anywhere.

Indian said, "I don't know what's going on, but something has spooked the people."

As they were passing the Cuero Bank & Trust, a teller stepped out of the bank and told them Kent Eagle and a man robbed the bank and rode down the street shooting at everything and everybody in sight.

Indian asked, "Where did they go after that, or do you know?" "I think they stopped at the saloon at the end of the street." Indian said, "Lightning, you and I are going in the front door of the saloon, and, Al, I want you to go around to the back of the saloon to be sure nobody comes out.

"If they do, shoot them and find out who they were later. Got that?"

"Got it, Boss!"

When Indian and Lightning arrived in front of the saloon, they saw two horses tied to the hitching rack.

They stopped their horses; then they slowly got off their horses and started into the saloon.

When they went through the swinging doors of the saloon, they saw the bartender standing behind the bar and one man sitting at a table by himself.

It didn't require much thought to understand what kind of man was sitting at the table. He looked like a poster for a gunslinger.

He had on a black hat and wore a fancy black vest with silver buttons and fringe over a black shirt; his two guns had white handle grips and were hanging low from his waist, resting in hand- tooled black leather holsters with a matching belt held together by a large silver belt buckle.

His black hair and black handlebar mustache set off his black eyes, which were watching every move Indian and Lightning made when they entered the saloon.

Indian walked to the bar and said, "Hello, Sam, how are you doing today?"

Sam slowly replied, "About as well as you would expect, considering the day."

"What do you mean, Sam?"

Before Sam could answer Indian, Lightning said, "What's your name, stranger?"

The gunslinger replied, "Not that it's any of your concern, but it's Mustang Jackson."

Lightning said, "I think I've heard of you. Don't you work for the back-shooting gambler called Eagle?"

"Maybe I do, and maybe I don't!"

"Where is that good-for-nothing, son of a bitch anyway?"

"Mister, what's your name? I want to be sure I have it for the book I keep with a list of the men I've killed. I want to be sure I get your name right!"

Lightning replied, "If I were you, I wouldn't be worried about getting my name right for your book. You just need to be sure I have your name right for your tombstone.

"If you really want to know the name of the man who's going to kill you, it's Lightning Cole."

Mustang Jackson stood up and started to draw his guns, but before he could clear the holsters with his guns, Lightning shot him first, right in the chest. Mustang fell to the floor, knocking the table over.

Lightning approached Mustang to see if he was dead, and when he leaned over, a bullet went over his head, missing him by maybe an inch.

Then Lightning heard two more shots, and he fell to the floor in time to see Kent Eagle falling over the rail from the second floor of the saloon; he then realized that Indian had just shot him.

When Indian and Lightning checked over the two men they had shot, they found both of them were dead.

Indian said, "I can't believe I killed Eagle with just two shots after all the problems he's caused the people of DeWitt County and Serene. I thought we would spend hours in a gun battle with him and his men, but after we killed so many of his men out at the Star Ranch, I guess the rest of them ran away.

"Sam, we'll get the undertaker to come and take this garbage out of here as soon as he can."

Indian took his sheriff's badge off and took off Lightning's deputy sheriff's badge off him and pinned the sheriff's badge on Lightning.

Indian said, "You're the sheriff now, Lightning, and you and Al will do a good job of keeping the peace around here. Don't you think so, Sam?"

"I sure as the hell think they will, and I'll tell Commissioner Swift that too."

Indian gave Lightning the keys to the sheriff's office and said, "It's all yours, Lightning, and if you ever need any help, you can call me."

Al came through the back door of the saloon and said, "Nobody came out so after I heard the shooting, I thought I better come in and check on you two."

Indian said, "Al, Lightning, has taken over my job as sheriff, so you're working for him now. Now, I'm going to go home to my bride and see what we're going to do about some place to live."

Al looked at Lightning and said, "You mean I have to work for you now?"

"You got it, Deputy. I'm sure you will do a fine job."

When Indian rode into the Star Ranch headquarters, he found Serene sitting in the cookhouse, drinking a cup of coffee.

Indian said, "Everything is all right now. Kent Eagle has been killed, and the rest of his men have run off. Now, what are we going to do for someplace to live, Serene?"

Serene replied, "Tonight we're sleeping in the cookhouse, and tomorrow we'll find someone to start building us a new home."

"That sounds good. I think I'm ready for a good night's sleep. "It's been quite a day, but I'm happy to say we don't have to worry anymore about the Phillips brothers or Kent Eagle, thank God."

They managed to get a good night's sleep on the floor of the cookhouse.

The next morning, Serene said, "Indian, I've been thinking, and I have an idea that when we build our new house, I want a bathroom built like the one we had in our honeymoon suite in Kansas City.

"Another thing, I think we better have a nursery built next to our bedroom because I'm pretty sure we going to have a baby."

"Serene, that's wonderful! I love you so much."

Two days later, Indian received a telegram from Robert that read as follows:

> Indian, you and Serene are needed to come to New York City to be the best man and bridesmaid for Joan's and my wedding.
>
> Come soon! We can't wait too long. Joan was right. She can get her daddy to do anything she wants. I'm not president of one of his banks, but I have a nice job as head of his trading company, which I love and which I am good at.
>
> Robert and Joan

Indian said, "I hope you can get someone to start building our house because we're going to New York City for Joan and Robert's wedding."

Serene replied, "Damn, I can't get ahead of that girl. I married a cowboy, so now she's marrying a cowboy!

"I only hope she loves him as much as I love you!"

The End

CPSIA information can be obtained
at www.ICGtesting.com
Printed in the USA
LVHW032011130821
695221LV00006B/439

9 781951 020323